D1590947

ARKANSAS
ALGAE
MONSTERS

CHECK OUT SOME OF THESE CHILLING,

#1: The Michigan Mega-Monsters
#2: Ogres of Ohio
#3: Florida Fog Phantoms
#4: New York Ninjas
#5: Terrible Tractors of Texas
#6: Invisible Iguanas of Illinois
#7: Wisconsin Werewolves
#8: Minnesota Mall Mannequins
#9: Iron Insects Invade Indiana
#10: Missouri Madhouse
#11: Poisonous Pythons Paralyze Pennsylvania
#12: Dangerous Dolls of Delaware
#13: Virtual Vampires of Vermont
#14: Creepy Condors of California
#15: Nebraska Nightcrawlers
#16: Alien Androids Assault Arizona
#17: South Carolina Sea Creatures
#18: Washington Wax Museum
#19: North Dakota Night Dragons
#20: Mutant Mammoths of Montana
#21: Terrifying Toys of Tennessee
#22: Nuclear Jellyfish of New Jersey
#23: Wicked Velociraptors of West Virginia
#24: Haunting in New Hampshire
#25: Mississippi Megalodon
#26: Oklahoma Outbreak
#27: Kentucky Komodo Dragons
#28: Curse of the Connecticut Coyotes
#29: Oregon Oceanauts
#30: Vicious Vacuums of Virginia
#31: The Nevada Nightmare Novel
#32: Idaho Ice Beast
#33: Monster Mosquitoes of Maine
#34: Savage Dinosaurs of South Dakota
#35: Maniac Martians Marooned in Massachusetts
#36: Carnivorous Crickets of Colorado
#37: The Underground Undead of Utah
#38: The Wicked Waterpark of Wyoming
#39: Angry Army Ants Ambush Alabama
#40: Incredible Ivy of Iowa
#41: North Carolina Night Creatures
#42: Arctic Anacondas of Alaska
#43: Robotic Rodents Ravage Rhode Island
#44: Arkansas Algae Monsters

For best prices and complete selection of all titles in stock,

GREAT BOOKS BY JOHNATHAN RAND!

Johnathan Rand's
MICHIGAN CHILLERS

#1: Mayhem on Mackinac Island
#2: Terror Stalks Traverse City
#3: Poltergeists of Petoskey
#4: Aliens Attack Alpena
#5: Gargoyles of Gaylord
#6: Strange Spirits of St. Ignace
#7: Kreepy Klowns of Kalamazoo
#8: Dinosaurs Destroy Detroit
#9: Sinister Spiders of Saginaw
#10: Mackinaw City Mummies
#11: Great Lakes Ghost Ship
#12: AuSable Alligators
#13: Gruesome Ghouls of Grand Rapids
#14: Bionic Bats of Bay City
#15: Calumet Copper Creatures
#16: Catastrophe in Caseville
#17: A Ghostly Haunting in Grand Haven
#18: Sault Ste. Marie Sea Monsters
#19: Drummond Island Dogman
#20: Lair of the Lansing Leprechauns

NIGHTMARE NATION
THE STATE OF FEAR IS HERE

#1: Village of the Dolls
#2: Night of the Hodag

THE ADVENTURE CLUB

#1: Ghost in the Graveyard
#2: Ghost in the Grand
#3: The Haunted Schoolhouse

**American Chillers
Double Thrillers:**
*Vampire Nation &
Attack of the Monster Venus Melon*

For Teens:
PANDEMIA: A novel of the
bird flu and the end of the world
(written with Christopher Knight)

Freddie Fernortner
FEARLESS FIRST GRADER

#1: The Fantastic Flying Bicycle
#2: The Super-Scary Night-Thingy
#3: A Haunting We Will Go
#4: Freddie's Dog Walking Service
#5: The Big Box Fort
#6: Mr. Chewy's Big Adventure
#7: The Magical Wading Pool
#8: Chipper's Crazy Carnival
#9: Attack of the Dust Bunnies From Outer Space
#10: The Pond Monster
#11: Tadpole Trouble
#12: FrankenFreddie!
#13: Day of the Dinosaurs

**CREEPY CAMPFIRE CHILLERS
VOLUME 1 & VOLUME 2**

*(Spine-tingling audio stories written
and read aloud by Johnathan Rand on
two specially-priced compact discs!)*

DOLLAR STORE DANNY

#1: The Dangerous Dinosaur
#2: The Salt Shaker Spaceship
#3: The Crazy Crayons
#4: The Shampoo Shark Attack

order direct from the publisher at www.americanchillers.com

For 20 years, Johnathan Rand has thrilled readers of all ages with his terrorizing tales of horror and suspense!

"I think everyone in school is reading your books! There's a girl in my class who says that *MONSTER MOSQUITOES OF MAINE* gave her horrible nightmares for a week!"

-Garrett C., age 13, Idaho

"I just finished reading *DINOSAURS DESTROY DETROIT* for the fourth time! I love all your books but that one is my very favorite!"

-Corbin D., age 10, Michigan

"When you came to our school, everyone started reading your books, including me. I thought they were too scary, but they are sooooo cool!"

-Jasmine H., age 9, Florida

"After I finished *NEBRASKA NIGHTCRAWLERS*, I had to read every book we had in the library. But we don't have *IDAHO ICE BEAST* because a kid puked on it by accident."

-Will B., age 10, South Dakota

"*AMERICAN CHILLERS* is the greatest book series in the whole world!"

-Caitlyn J., age 12, Virginia

"I hope you never stop writing books. I used to hate reading, but now I love books. Especially yours!"

-Dante D., age 12, New York

"I love your books and I love to write, too! I want to come to your writing camp next summer!"

-Patricia B., age 11, Ohio

"My favorite thing to do in the whole world is read your books in bed with the lights off! Well, I have a flashlight so I can read. But all the other lights are off, and I always creep myself out!"

-Mark K., age 10, Texas

"My sister gave me a couple of your books for my birthday, and I LOVE them, especially *NORTH DAKOTA NIGHT DRAGONS*!"

-Riley S., age 8, Michigan

"Thank you for writing these books. I like your weird glasses. I like your dogs. I like your dogs better than your glasses. But I like your books the best."

-Harper A., age 11, Tennessee

"Have you ever thought of making movies out of your books? That would be awesome! I love your books, but I think they would make super-cool movies!"

-Rick L., age 12, Oregon

"I started reading the *AMERICAN CHILLERS* series two years ago, and I've read them all! They're GREAT!"

-Ian M., age 13, Illinois

"After I read *DANGEROUS DOLLS OF DELAWARE*, I had nightmares for weeks. Good job!"

-Kim P., age 12, California

"Thank you for signing my books when I came to your signing at the bookstore! I got three new books, too!"

-Carter R., age 9, Indiana

"I read *THE MICHIGAN MEGA-MONSTERS* in one day because it was so good! Keep writing and I will keep reading. Promise!"

-Hannah.G., age 11, California

"Can you write a book and put my name in it? I think that would be cool and I would buy it and read it. Please think seriously about this. I LOVE your books forever!"

-Tanner S., age 10, Missouri

"Everyone at our school loved your assembly! I hope you can come back soon! I learned a lot and now I want to be an author. Come back! Don't forget!"

-Brandon B., age 10, Nevada

"My most favorite book I have ever read is *WICKED VELOCIRAPTORS OF WEST VIRGINIA*. I hope you make more dinosaur books. I will read all of them!"

-Preston A., age 10, Wisconsin

"How do you get all your scary and crazy ideas? I tried writing my own scary story, and it's really hard."

-Kathy L., age 8, Utah

Love Johnathan Rand's books? Let us know! Drop us a note, and you might see your quote in an upcoming book! Send it to:

Chillers Blurbs
281 Cool Blurbs Ave
Topinabee, MI 49791

#44: Arkansas Algae Monsters

Johnathan Rand

An AudioCraft Publishing, Inc., book

This book is a work of fiction. Names, places, characters and incidents are used fictitiously, or are part of the author's very active imagination.

Book storage and warehousing provided by *Chillermania*, 1651 South Straits Hwy., Indian River, Michigan 49749

No part of this published work may be reproduced in whole or in part, by any means, without written permission from the publisher. For information regarding permissions, contact: AudioCraft Publishing, Inc., PO Box 281, Topinabee Island, MI 49791

American Chillers #44: *Arkansas Algae Monsters*

ISBN: 978-1-942950-00-4

Librarians/Media Specialists: PCIP/MARC records available **free of charge** at www.americanchillers.com

Cover illustration by Dwayne Harris

Cover layout by Sue Harring

Printed in USA

ARKANSAS ALGAE MONSTERS

VISIT CHILLERMANIA!

WORLD HEADQUARTERS FOR BOOKS BY JOHNATHAN RAND!

Visit the HOME for books by Johnathan Rand! Featuring books, hats, shirts, bookmarks and other cool stuff not available anywhere else in the world! Plus, watch the American Chillers website for news of special events and signings at *CHILLERMANIA!* with author Johnathan Rand! Located in northern lower Michigan, on I-75! Take exit 313 . . . then south 1 mile! For more info, call (231) 238-0338. And be afraid! Be veeeery afraaaaaaiiiid . . . .

1

Nothing exciting ever happens in Russellville, Arkansas.

Nothing.

Now, I'm not saying that the town is *always* boring, because it's really not. I have a lot of fun, and so do my friends. We make our own fun.

But Russellville is a lot like most other small towns in Arkansas, with friendly people who treat everyone like family or neighbors. It can be boring at times, but I think you can be bored no matter where you live. And it doesn't have anything to do with the town you live in.

My name is Olivia Barner, and I'm twelve. My friends call me 'Liv' or sometimes 'Livie.' Dad sometimes calls me 'Livie Bean,' and it drives me crazy.

It makes me sound like I'm five years old.

But this isn't a story about me. Well, I guess it is in one way, because it happened to me. But it's also a story about how sometimes, even in small American towns, things can go from boring to exciting in the blink of an eye.

On the day everything happened I was eating lunch with Mom. My older brother, Travis, was at work. He's sixteen and has a job working at old man Miller's farm a few miles away.

And Dad? Dad is a long-haul trucker, so he's sometimes gone for weeks at a time. He'd called Mom earlier that particular morning to let her know he was in Des Moines, Iowa, and hoped to make it home in about a week.

"Try this, Olivia," Mom said. "It's a new chili recipe I'm trying out."

Mom placed a bowl of steaming goop on the table in front of me. She's a good cook, and she's always coming up with new recipes and different ways to cook things. She can make a homemade pizza that is better than anything you can buy in any restaurant.

"Chili?" I asked, picking up a spoon.

"Spicy," she said with a nod and a smile. "Try

it."

She wasn't kidding. The chili was not only *hot*...it had a spice to it that singed my tongue!

And I *loved* it.

"This is great!" I said.

Mom smiled. "I thought you'd like that," she said. "I'll save some for Travis when he gets home. And I'll make a new batch for your father, too. I think he'll really like it."

"It's great," I said. "Hot. Really, really hot!"

I took a sip of water and put the glass down.

"What are you up to the rest of the day?" Mom asked.

I scooped up another spoonful of chili and paused.

"I don't know," I said with a shrug. "Max is coming over. We might go to the park if it doesn't rain."

Mom glanced out the window. "It's been looking like it might rain all morning," she said. "I checked the—"

Mom's sentence was interrupted by a thundering, distant crash. The windows rattled.

"What was that?!" I asked, getting to my feet.

Mom and I rushed to the kitchen window. Our faces nearly touched the glass.

We both gasped at the same time.

What had been a very ordinary day was about to get really, really strange.

And scary.

2

Mom skirted around the dining room table and snapped up her phone from the counter.

"I'll call the police," she said.

While she punched in the number, I raced through the kitchen and out the front door. In a few giant, bounding steps I cleared the porch and was running down the driveway and out to the street.

In the distance, I could see the scene of the accident. A large, white, box truck was on its side. Black and gray smoke was roiling and curling into the air, creating a dark balloon.

I hope no one is hurt, I thought, as my shoes slapped the pavement.

I snapped my head around to make sure no cars were coming up behind me. We live in a rural area a few miles from Russellville, and there aren't very many homes nearby. Likewise, there isn't very much traffic. But the road we live on connects to Interstate 40, so cars and trucks often use our road to get to the freeway.

As I ran, my eyes scanned the scene. Questions whirled in my head, and I tried to figure out what had happened, and what to do when I reached the accident.

The first thing, I knew, was to make sure no one was hurt.

But then what? I wondered. *What if someone is hurt really bad?*

I didn't know what I could do. I've never been hurt bad myself. Once, I cut my arm on a piece of metal. The wound bled really bad, and I needed fifteen stitches. I still have a scar from my forearm to my elbow.

But this was different. This was a truck accident. There might be someone hurt a lot worse than I had been.

Maybe someone had even been—

No, Olivia, I told myself. *Don't even think about it.*

I continued to run toward the overturned truck. I didn't see any other vehicle, so it didn't appear as though there had been a collision. That was good, I thought, as the fewer people involved, the better.

But who was driving the truck? Was he—or she—okay? Were they still inside the vehicle? Maybe they were stuck inside and couldn't get out?

My shoes smacked the pavement, matching the beating of my racing heart. My long hair flew behind me, trailing like fire.

And ahead of me, at the scene of the accident, smoke continued to billow up, to fill the sky, a growing mushroom of black and gray.

"Is everyone okay?!" I yelled, approaching the scene. "Is anybody hurt?!"

I slowed and stopped before I reached the truck. Now that I was closer, I could see that the hood of the truck had popped open. It was bent and twisted, and smoke was coming from the engine. Thankfully, I didn't see any flames.

"Hello?" I shouted. "Can anyone hear me?"

The windshield was shattered but intact in a

tightly knitted spider web pattern.

But nearby, I saw something that nearly caused my heart to stop.

Laying on the ground near the truck was a bicycle.

It was blue.

It had a black leather seat.

There was a black satchel attached to the handlebars.

I knew—instantly—the bike belonged to my friend, Max.

3

Although the day was hot and muggy, a chill iced my skin. I froze. It felt as though my bones, joints, and muscles had locked up, making it impossible to move. Everything around me seemed to be moving in slow motion: the bicycle tire, the black, chalky smoke billowing up from the engine at the front of the overturned truck. It was like time was slowing down.

Finally, I managed to speak.

"Max?" I said. I intended to yell his name, but the word came out more like a croak.

There was no response.

"Max?" I said again. A bit louder this time, and not so croaky.

With every passing second, the knot in my gut twisted. The chill on my skin seeped into my muscles, and I knew something horrible had happened to my friend.

I finally found the strength to move, making my way around the front of the truck.

I heard a voice.

"Hello?" I said. "Is everyone okay?"

"Olivia? Is that you?"

Max!

I hurried around the front of the truck to find Max standing next to a man I didn't know. The man was wearing blue denim overalls and a blue shirt with a company logo stitched in white over the right front pocket. He held a phone to his ear.

"Olivia!" Max said, rushing to me.

"Are you okay?" I asked. "What happened?"

Max turned and hiked his thumb in the direction of the man holding the phone to his ear.

"I'm not sure," he said. "But I think he took the turn too fast. Or wasn't paying attention. Or both. He went off the shoulder of the road and must've over-corrected or something. His truck flipped onto its side."

"Was there anyone else in the truck?" I asked.

Max shook his head. "No," he said. "Just him. He said he had his seat belt on, so he was pretty lucky."

"I saw your bike over there," I said, pointing. "I thought something terrible had happened."

"I was on my way to your house. I was back there—" he said, pointing down the road, "—and I heard the crash. If I had been looking in that direction, I would've seen the truck flip. By the time I got here, the guy had already climbed out of the cab. He's on the phone talking to the police right now."

"I'm glad he's okay," I said. "You, too. If you had been closer, and he hadn't been paying attention...."

Max nodded. "I thought of that, too. But I'm okay. Everything is fine."

But Max was wrong. Everything was not fine. In fact, everything was about to turn very, very bad.

Max and I stood in silence for a moment. The man who'd been driving the truck was still on the phone, although we couldn't hear what he was saying.

Farther down the road, I saw Mom's car pull out of the driveway.

"Here comes my mom," I said.

She stopped her car on the shoulder of the road and got out. Max and I hurried up to her, and we quickly explained what had happened. Mom listened carefully, eyes wide. She was relieved when I told her no one had been hurt.

"You and Max come on home," she said. "The police will be here soon, and they'll get things straightened out."

Mom turned her car around and went back to our house.

"Grab your bike," I said. Max walked to his bike and picked it up.

"Hey!" someone shouted in the distance.

We turned to see the man—the driver—waving to us. He was no longer talking on his phone.

Max and I walked up to him, Max pushing his bike.

The man stuck out his hand and Max shook it. "I just wanted to say thank you for stopping to check on me," he said. He frowned thoughtfully. "This could have been a lot worse."

"I'm glad you're okay," Max said. "But your truck is going to need some work."

"Yeah," the man said.

"What's that?" I asked, pointing to a silver cylinder on its side. It was about the size and shape of the propane tank Dad uses for our gas grill, but this one had a lid that had broken open. A dark green substance had spilled out, oozing onto the shoulder of the road. The canister must have fallen out when the truck rolled onto its side.

The man shook his head. "Yeah," he said. "That's too bad. Nothing hazardous, though."

"What's in it?" Max asked.

"Algae," the man replied.

I frowned. "Algae? Like the kind of algae in dirty fish tanks?"

The man shrugged. "I guess so," he said. "But I'm not really sure. It was some sort of experiment. I guess it was normal algae that was sent into space by NASA."

My jaw dropped. "Sent into space?"

"So, it's space algae?" Max asked.

The man scratched his head. "No, not quite," he said. "I guess some high school kids in Michigan came up with some experimental test and won a contest that NASA was putting on. The kids wanted to see what would happen to the algae in an environment without gravity and oxygen."

"What happened to it?" I asked.

The man shrugged and shook his head. "I couldn't tell you. Probably nothing. That's where that container was headed: back up to Michigan so the kids could finish their experiment. But not all the algae spilled out, so it's not a total loss. Got lots of other stuff

I'm hauling in the truck, too. Good thing nothing else got busted open."

"Do you need any help?" Max asked.

"Nah," the man said. "Cops will be here pretty quick. And a wrecker. Not sure what I'm going to do with all the things I'm hauling, though. Probably have to rent another truck. But I'll figure it out."

"Okay," I said.

"Thanks again," the man said.

Max and I turned and began walking toward my house. Max held the handlebars of his bike, pushing it alongside him.

"Algae in space," Max said with a snicker. "Who comes up with this stuff?"

"Some high school kids, I guess," I replied.

"Seems like a waste of time," Max said. "But you have to admit: space algae sounds like the beginning of a great science fiction book or movie."

"Evil space algae," I said with a laugh. "Evil space algae that attacks people and takes over the world."

Max laughed. "It might make a great book," he said.

"But it could never happen," I replied.

Later, when everything did start to happen, when I realized the danger we were all in, I would remember those words.

It could never happen.

But it did.

Everything in my world was about to get really, really crazy.

5

As exciting as the truck rollover was, I forgot about it pretty quick. For a vehicle accident, it hadn't been all that serious, and I was glad. The truck driver had been lucky. It hadn't been long before the police showed up, as well as an ambulance. The ambulance had been just a precaution. From my house, I saw it arrive in a swarm of flashing red lights. After the paramedics found that no one had been injured, they left. This time, however, their flashing emergency lights were off. I don't remember a tow truck showing up because I got busy doing other things. However, by suppertime, the overturned truck was gone. Looking up the road, it looked perfectly normal, like nothing had even happened.

But in the ground at the scene of the accident, lots of things were happening. I just didn't know it yet.

That evening, it was just Mom and me for supper. Dad was still on the road, of course. Travis, was working a double shift at Miller's farm and wouldn't be home until late.

"I don't want you to get sick of my chili," Mom said as she put a bowl on the dining room table. "But that's what we've got. It's hot, so be careful."

"Dad will love it," I said. "Dad loves spicy stuff."

"I'm using the peppers I've been growing in the garden," Mom said. "Not very many of them, either. A little bit goes a long way."

Mom had been growing a strain of peppers called Arkansas Night Reapers. She heard about them through a friend of hers, who gave her the seeds. The peppers are supposed to be hot—dangerously hot—and if you're not careful, you could wind up in the hospital. That is, of course, if you ate them raw. Arkansas Night Reapers are all black with dark red blotches. They even *look* dangerous. Mom was careful to warn Travis and me never to eat any, that they were grown especially to add to food. She said that someone in Little Rock had eaten several of the peppers on a dare last summer, and they had to be taken to the hospital by ambulance, where they almost died. But, Mom said, the peppers were perfectly fine—delicious, in fact—when used in small amounts as a spice for food.

I stirred the chili in my bowl and scooped up a spoonful. After blowing on it, I carefully put the spoon in my mouth. The chili was tasty, but it was also super hot. But I noticed that the heat quickly went away, and the only thing left was a delicious, spicy taste.

"It's really good," I said, and I repeated: "Dad is going to *love* this. Travis, too."

"Good," Mom said, placing her own bowl on the table and sitting. "I have enough of those Arkansas Night Reapers that I'm going to be able to can them and save them. Just a few of them will go a long way. What's your friend Max up to? How's he doing?"

"He's fine," I said. "He's going to come over tomorrow and we're going to go to Shiloh Park to goof around."

"That'll be fun," Mom said.

And it was.

Max rode his bike to our house the next

morning, and I hopped on my bike. We rode together to Shiloh Park, which is only a couple of miles from where we live.

Shiloh Park is really cool. It's big, too, and lots of people use it, including many of my friends from school. There are two softball fields including some bleachers, so when games are being played, people can watch. There are even lights so games can be played after dark. There are also a couple of tennis courts and a play area for kids, which is pretty cool. And Shiloh Park borders Lake Dardanelle, which is a great fishing lake. A few years ago, Travis caught a huge largemouth bass that weighed a whopping fifteen pounds, which was almost the state record! Travis' picture was on the front page of the local newspaper, grinning and holding up the huge fish.

But we didn't go to Shiloh Park to fish. Mostly, we would meet friends there and hang out, or, like today, simply toss a Frisbee back and forth. The park has a big field with plenty of room for us and anyone else who wants to play.

When we took a break, Max and I walked over to the pavilion where there's a drinking fountain. The water was cool and fresh, and I gulped it down.

Nearby, there were a couple of moms watching their young kids playing on the swings, and I couldn't help but to overhear their conversation. I didn't really pay attention because it's rude to eavesdrop on people like that, but I heard one of the moms say something that caught my attention.

"It was back there," the woman said, turning and pointing. "We were driving here, and the thing was on the side of the road."

"And it was green?" the other mom said.

"Yeah," the woman replied. "Just a green blob, on the side of the highway. And I swear it was moving! Out of the corner of my eye, I thought it might have been a dog or something. But it wasn't."

"So, what was it?" the other mom asked.

The other woman shook her head. "I'm not sure," she said. "We passed, and when I looked in the mirror, it was gone."

"That's really weird," the woman said.

Max had been getting a drink at the water fountain, and we walked back to the field together.

"Did you hear that?" I asked.

"Hear what?"

"That woman back there," I replied. "She said

she saw some sort of...something. A green blob, on the side of the highway."

"She was seeing things," Max said.

"Maybe," I replied. "But she was pointing in the direction of my house."

"Like I said," Max repeated, "she was seeing things. Hey. I'm hungry. Let's get something to eat."

"Want some of my mom's killer chili?" I asked.

"That sounds great!" Max replied.

Now, at the time, we had no idea that anything could possibly be wrong. We had no idea that the crashed truck from the day before, and, in particular, the spilled algae, was going to cause the horrifying situation we would find ourselves in. Even the fact that the woman at the park said she saw a 'green blob' didn't really concern me.

It should have.

6

We hopped on our bikes and rode from Shiloh Park to my house in the hot, mid-day sun. Arkansas gets pretty steamy and humid during the summer months—much hotter than the northern states. And although the winters can get a little chilly, we don't get much snow like they do in the northern part of the country. Not where we live, anyway. Once in a while, we might get a dusting of snow or maybe some ice. But not very often.

Our home is in the middle of a huge field. Dad said that it used to be a farm a long time ago, but when he and Mom bought it, no one had grown anything there for years. Mom has a big garden and grows vegetables and flowers. The closest other house is across the road and on the other side of a field. From our house, you can barely see it. Dad and Mom said they like living where we do because it's private, but I think it can be pretty boring sometimes. Thankfully, I have a bike and can ride to my friends' houses or to Shiloh Park. Or into town, where I can hang out with my friends.

When we got to our home there was a note on the counter from Mom saying that she was out running errands, would be back later in the afternoon, and to call her if I needed anything. I have my own phone which is pretty cool, but it doesn't have any games or connect to the Internet. It's just a simple phone. Mom's note went on to say that I could make a sandwich or have some chili that was on low heat in a huge Crock Pot.

"Why is it called a 'Crock Pot?'" Max asked after glancing at Mom's note.

"Mom says it's a brand name. It's actually just a slow cooker. Lots of different companies make them, but the term 'Crock Pot' has been around since it was invented."

"It's a funny name," Max said.

"Yeah," I said. "Here." I placed a bowl of chili on the table in front of Max. "And be careful eating this stuff. Mom uses Arkansas Night Reaper peppers to spice it up, and it'll set your mouth on fire."

We finished our chili, then played a few video games. Mom called once to check on us and see how her chili was doing in the slow cooker. Other than that? It was a pretty normal afternoon.

That was about to change.

"I gotta be getting home," Max said, glancing at the clock on the wall. It was nearing three in the afternoon. "Mom says we have to go to some wedding reception." He rolled his eyes. "She says I have to get cleaned up and wear nice clothes ánd stuff."

"Well," I said, "it is a wedding. You don't want to go looking like that." I nodded at him, and he looked down. He was wearing red shorts and a gray T-shirt, and his knees were dirty.

He smiled. "Yeah, I guess not," he said. "Anyway. You wanna go back to the park tomorrow? We can take our fishing poles and maybe do some fishing."

"That sounds great," I said. "I have to catch a bigger bass than my brother. Anytime anyone talks

37

about fishing, he starts yapping about that big bass he caught a couple of years ago, and how it almost broke the state record."

Max and I walked outside. His helmet was on his bicycle seat, and he put it on.

"See ya," he said, as he hopped on his bike.

"See ya," I replied with a wave.

Max rode off, and I returned to the house. It was still early in the day, and I started thinking of things to do. Mom wanted me to keep an eye on her chili and stir it once in a while, so that was the first thing on my list.

I never made it to the kitchen. Before I'd even closed the front door, I was stopped by a shrill, piercing scream in the distance. There was no question who it was.

Max.

7

I spun and stood in the doorway. Max had been riding along the shoulder of the road. Now, however, he wasn't on his bicycle. From what I could see, it appeared his bike was on its side, on the shoulder. Max, too, was on the shoulder of the road, but it appeared that he was partially in the ditch, as the only portion of him that I could see of him was from his waist up.

But without question, even from the distance and the shimmering heat waves, I could see that he was in distress. He was struggling with something and screaming for help.

My bike was in the driveway and I raced to it,

not even taking the time to put on my helmet. I grabbed the handlebars and swung onto the seat in one single motion, pedaling furiously, my legs pumping as I charged down the driveway.

What was wrong? I wondered. *What could have happened?*

Max was still on the side of the road and partially in the ditch. He saw me coming and he'd stopped yelling, but I could see that he was still struggling.

It took me less than a minute to reach him. I skidded to a stop on the gravel, leaping from my bike and letting it fall to the ground.

"Max!" I shouted. "Max!" What's wrong?!?!"

"My foot!" he wailed. "The green stuff won't let go!"

Green stuff? I thought. *What's he talking about?*

When I reached him, he had both hands on his left thigh, using them to try to pull his foot away. It was as though his leg was caught in a trap, and he was struggling to get free.

"Help me get my foot out of this stuff!" he said.

His dirty white sneaker was caught in some sort of dark green gel. It was stretchy but it was strong; not like a mud puddle or anything like that. This was like some sort of goopy glue, and it completely covered his shoe.

"Give me your hand!" I shouted. Max let go of his leg with one hand, reaching out. I took it with both hands and took a step back, using my body weight to leverage against Max and whatever it was that was gripping his foot. I leaned back, pulling as hard as I could.

"Hold on!" I shouted.

"Pull harder!" Max yelled.

It's that algae, I thought. *It's that algae that spilled from that container when that guy rolled his truck. But how did it get here? The truck accident was farther down the road, a hundred yards from here. How did the algae get this far away?*

At the moment, that didn't matter. What mattered was that Max's foot was caught, and he couldn't get it unstuck.

Finally, we succeeded...but not necessarily in the way we intended.

Without warning, Max and I tumbled backward. We both lost our balance and our footing and fell to the ground. I was filled with relief.

"That thing got my shoe!" Max hollered.

We got to our feet and walked to where the pile of green goop was. Max's foot had come out of his sneaker, and—here's the really weird part—it was being eaten! The green goop was chewing Max's shoe! It was as though the green goop was alive, slowly chewing Max's shoe, devouring it completely.

"What...what is that stuff?" Max said. His voice was tense, serious.

"I think it's that algae that spilled when that guy flipped his truck," I said.

"But that was way up there," Max said, pointing and looking up and off into the distance. "This isn't anywhere close to where he rolled his truck. How did the algae get here?"

At the moment, that wasn't the biggest question on my mind. I was too focused on what the blob of algae was doing to Max's shoe.

Max reached down, but I grabbed his arm and spoke.

"Don't do that," I said. "It might grab your hand."

"It's not a rattlesnake," Max said.

"No, it's not," I said. "Maybe it's worse."

We stood in the afternoon sun, looking down. A car approached on the highway, slowing as it reached us. Stopped. A man was driving, and there was a woman in the passenger's seat. The passenger's side window was down.

"Everything okay?" the woman asked.

"Yeah," I said.

"We saw the bikes on the shoulder," she said. "We thought you might be in trouble."

"Not yet," Max replied.

Not yet, I thought. *That's an odd thing to say.*

"We're fine," I said. "Thanks for stopping, though."

The man and woman smiled, waved, and drove off.

"It's gone," Max said. "That thing ate my whole shoe."

He was right. The green blob was still on the ground, but Max's shoe was completely gone. It was though the entire sneaker had disintegrated.

Not only that, but while we watched, the dark green blob became smaller. It didn't take us long to realize it was seeping into the ground. In less than a minute, the goop had vanished, leaving only trace

43

amounts of residue on the gravel and dirt.

"There's something really, really wrong about this," I said quietly.

"That thing ate my shoe," Max repeated.

"Be thankful it didn't eat your foot," I replied.

"What am I going to tell my mom about my shoe?" Max asked.

"Tell her the truth," I said. "Tell her that your shoe was eaten by a ball of green slime."

"She's going to think I'm crazy."

"Then she'll have to think I'm crazy, too," I said. "I saw the same thing you did."

I watched Max pedal off on his bike. He looked funny, with only one shoe and one sock.

I looked down at the ground. Except for the tiny traces of green that splattered the ground, there was no trace of the glob that had eaten Max's shoe.

I was puzzled and confused. But what's more: I was worried. There was a growing fear within me, a knotted fist in my stomach that felt tight and uncomfortable. Something was wrong. It was as though something was coming, something that threatened to invade my world and the safety of my average, ordinary life.

I would soon find out that I was right.

8

Summertime in Russellville, Arkansas, is like a dream. Sure, it's hot and humid, but I'd rather have that than have to deal with the frozen arctic tundra of some of the northern states. Russellville isn't a big city, and people are friendly. I have a lot of friends at school, although I don't see too many of them until classes begin again in September. Dad used to live in Little Rock, which is much bigger than Russellville. He says Little Rock is great, but he and Mom prefer the small town feel of Russellville. Sure, it can be a little boring sometimes, but I always seem to find some things to do, especially during the summer. Travis works, Dad travels across the country, and Mom tends to her garden. She works at a department store a couple of days a week, too. But she loves her garden, and she loves cooking and baking.

"I'm making more chili for the church potluck this weekend," she said as I strode into the kitchen. This was the following day, the day after the truck had rolled over, the day after the mysterious green glob ate Max's shoe. I'd told Mom about it, but she said that it was probably some sort of chemical effect and that I should probably stay away from it if I saw it again. She said that if we did happen to see it again, we should probably report it, as it might be toxic.

However, I didn't think we'd see it again. I figured that, whatever it was, it had seeped into the ground and was gone for good.

"The chili smells good," I said.

"I'm going to work today," Mom continued. "Travis says he's working another double shift, so he won't be home until late. I'll need you to hang around the house and check on the slow cooker every once in a while."

"Can I go to the park with Max?" I asked.

"Sure," Mom said. "Just come back to check on the chili. I'm going to be cooking it on 'high' for the first few hours, and I want you to drop it to the 'low' setting at around three o'clock or so."

"Okay."

"Oh," Mom said. She pointed to my phone on the counter. "JoJo called you this morning. She wants you to call her back."

JoJo is another friend from school. She lives on the other side of Shiloh Park, and I've known her forever. In the summer, we hang out a lot together. JoJo is probably the kindest person I know.

After breakfast, I called JoJo back. She was all excited to tell me about her new bicycle, and how cool and fast it was.

"Why don't you ride your bike over here this afternoon so I can see it?" I asked. "Max is coming over, and I know he'll want to see it, too. Then we can all go to the park."

"That sounds great," she said. "Wait until you see my bike!"

"I'm excited!" I said. "I can't wait!"

"See you later today!"

I went into my room to read a book, but I couldn't focus on the story. My thoughts kept drifting back to the day before: the truck accident, the green algae, and, more specifically, that weird green blob that ate Max's shoe. There was something really wrong with that. Even if it was some sort of chemical-like goop, it shouldn't have seeped into the ground and vanished like it did. That just seemed really bizarre.

So, I gave up reading and decided to go have another look at the place where Max lost his shoe. I didn't know exactly what I was looking for, and I didn't know what I would find. Probably nothing, but I was curious. I wanted to see the place again. I wanted to see if we missed something the day before.

I was tying my shoes when Mom hollered.

"I'm off to work," she said. "Don't forget to stir my chili."

"I won't," I called back from my bedroom. Have a good day."

It was just before noon. I wasn't sure exactly when Max was coming over, but I knew it would be soon. And JoJo? She would be riding over later.

I went outside and pushed my bike off the porch. The day was hot, and the air was thick. The sky was overcast. When clouds cover the sky, it can get really muggy and uncomfortable. I kept asking Dad if he would get us a pool for the back yard, but he only laughed and said, 'suck it up, buttercup.' Whatever that meant. I guess it was his way of saying he wasn't going to buy us a pool.

I rode up the driveway and turned on to the shoulder of the road, my tires grinding on the hard-packed gravel along the ditch. I kept my eyes open for anything strange, but I didn't see anything.

When I reached the place where Max had lost his shoe, I stopped. I propped my bike up on the kickstand, then slowly walked around, looking down, scanning and searching.

What am I looking for? I asked myself. *Something green? Max's shoe?*

I had no clue. I really didn't think I'd find anything...but I was curious, just the same.

A car went by, and I watched it pass.

I continued scouring the ground, looking for anything, searching for some of the green stuff we'd seen yesterday, the gelatin-like substance that had latched on to Max's foot. I found nothing. Not a single trace.

Weird, I thought.

After a few minutes of searching, I gave up. Whatever it had been, it was gone—just like Max's shoe.

I walked back to my bike, still leaning on its kickstand on the shoulder of the road at the edge of the drainage ditch. On the other side of the ditch, the land sloped up; there was a small area of grass and then a forest. As I was putting my helmet on, a slight movement drew my attention to the woods.

I turned.

Something moved.

I saw branches waver and bend.

More movement.

Something...green.

I froze. I'd just fastened the strap of my bike helmet, and I held the nylon in my fingers, my hands just beneath my chin.

I watched.

A bead of sweat formed on my forehead and trickled down my nose. Slowly, I wiped it away with my finger.

I continued looking for movement, but I didn't see anything. The branches stilled, and whatever had caused them to move was gone.

What was it? What had caused the branches to move? A deer?

No. It had been green. I was sure of it. Deer aren't green.

The memory of yesterday, of Max's foot caught in the green goop and the struggle to free it flooded back to me. I hadn't been scared when that happened.

Now, I was feeling a ticking of fear inside. Something green had moved in the woods not far away. It hadn't been very big, but it was enough to cause branches to bobble and bend.

And I also knew something else: if I didn't find out what it was, I would always wonder what it had been. I would forever kick myself for not investigating, for not being brave enough to check it out.

I unsnapped my helmet, lifted it off my head, and placed it on my bike seat. I looked both ways on the highway; no one was coming. Not that it mattered. But somehow, the empty road made me feel more alone. By myself.

On my own.

Again, I glanced into the forest.

Nothing moved.

Still—

I pushed away fearful thoughts. Inside, I laughed at my fear. I knew that little voice was lying to me. That little voice was just trying to scare me, frighten me off. The little voice of fear was making things up, making my imagination go crazy.

That's what I told myself.

I was about to find out that the little voice was telling the truth.

9

I carefully made my way down the short embankment. The bottom of the drainage ditch had a small amount of water in it, but I was able to leap over it easily and climb the slope on the other side. At the top of the ditch I stopped, again searching the woods.

Nothing.

But I had spotted something, I was sure.

I made my way to the edge of the forest, scanning back and forth, my eyes tracking from side to side.

There.

Another movement.

Just a slight disturbance of a tree branch, a

gentle bobbing of a limb. But it hadn't been the wind, I was sure. Something had caused the branch to bend.

Slowly, I made my way through the woods, pushing branches out of my way, keeping my attention focused on the place where I'd spotted the movement.

Something else I noticed: my fear had left me. I no longer felt frightened. I wasn't scared, not at all. Curious, yes. But not scared. I knew that there was some sort of explanation for what I'd seen. There was something in the forest, sure...but I knew I would discover some animal, a small deer or perhaps something even smaller like a raccoon. A bear? Unlikely. We have black bears in Arkansas, but you don't see them very often. Besides, if a bear had caused the branches to move, I would have spotted the animal by now.

Then, up ahead, I spotted something.

Something green.

It was about the size of a beach ball, and it was difficult to make out because it blended with the surrounding vegetation.

Still pushing branches and limbs away, I pressed on, closer and closer to the blob of—

What? Algae?

I had no idea...but I was going to find out.

In a few more steps, I'd reached the blob. Slowly, I pushed more limbs away so I could see it better.

My curiosity was in overdrive as I inspected the mysterious green object on the ground, nearly hidden among the leafy foliage. But as I stared at it more and more, that little twitch of fear, that little elf of fright that lives inside of me, began to whisper again. Warning me, telling me that I'd better be careful, better leave now, better get away....

Is this the same thing that had eaten Max's shoe? I wondered. It sure looked like it. It was bigger, so maybe it was a different one.

A different one...of *what?*

I picked up a dead stick. Carefully, I knelt down and poked the green blob. The gel gave way to it, like soft rubber.

I poked harder. Maybe if I pushed hard enough, the stick would pierce the blob and some sort of jelly would spill out. That would be gross.

A crow called from nearby, startling me. I didn't see it, nor did I take my eyes off the green blob before me.

I pushed harder with the stick.

Suddenly, as if a mouth had opened up, the green gel took hold of the branch. Stunned, I stood up and took a step back.

The green blob began to chew the stick!

I took another step back, watching the blob munch on the branch, slowly devouring it, chewing like a cow eating grass. It was the most bizarre thing I'd ever seen in my life. At that moment, the blob seemed alive, animated, like it was some sort of animal without arms or legs.

Or maybe a reptile or amphibian, I thought. At school, we'd learned all about those two classifications of animals. Reptiles have bodies made of scales or shells, like snakes, crocodiles, and turtles. They live mostly on land. Amphibians rely on water and spend much of their lives living in the aquatics, being that their skin is porous and they need the moisture in order to live. Sometimes, people confuse the two classifications. Some people think turtles are amphibians, but they're not. And some people think frogs are reptiles. At school, one of our assignments had been to create a poster listing five reptiles and five amphibians, and what qualities each possessed that classified them as such. Max and I worked on that project together, and we got an 'A.'

But the blob in front of me? I wasn't sure what it was. Reptile? Amphibian? Plant?

I had no idea. The only thing I knew was that, as I watched, the stick became smaller and smaller as the green blob devoured it. When it was gone, the blob stopped moving.

The crow called out again.

On the highway, a car passed by, its tires droning on the pavement.

Then, before my eyes, the blob began to grow. It moved slowly, as if there was something inside it, trying to come out.

It inched toward me.

Then, without any warning whatsoever, the green blob came at me.

10

My reflexes immediately took over. Before I knew it, I was running—as fast as I could, anyway, considering I was in the woods—throwing branches out of my way. Limbs scratched my arms and neck, and I had to duck down and dart around trees. When I did manage to glance back, the green glob was in pursuit, moving amazingly fast.

Questions drilled at my mind. *What is it? Where did it come from? What did it want? Why was it coming after me?*

Those were all questions that would have to wait. The only thing I cared about at that moment was getting away, getting out of the woods, getting on my bike, and pedaling home as fast as I could. When I was safely in the house, I could call Mom. She would come home, but in the meantime, she would tell me to stay inside and lock the doors, then call the police.

If, of course, I actually *made* it home.

I emerged from the forest. Running was easier now, and I sprinted through the tall grass. A car drove by on the highway, but the two occupants in the front seat were staring straight ahead, and they never saw me.

I bounded down the drainage ditch, leaped over the small stretch of water, and scrambled up the other side.

Behind me, the blob was hobbling through the grass. And was I imagining things, or did it look bigger than it had, even moments ago? I wasn't sure. But it appeared to be larger. Not only that, it appeared to be oddly humanoid. Large and round, yes, probably about half my height and twice as wide. But it sure looked like it had a head. And arms, too. And legs. It was the most bizarre thing I'd ever seen in my life.

I made it to my bike and quickly put my helmet over my head. No time to latch the strap; I simply leapt onto my bike, turned it around, and began pedaling, flying down the shoulder of the road.

Behind me, the green blob was at the side of the drainage ditch. It was no longer pursuing me, but standing at the top of the embankment. Although it didn't have eyes, it appeared as though it was watching me. In fact, I was certain it was watching me. It appeared to be disappointed that it had missed me, missed its chance to—

—*to what? I wondered. What did it want? Did it want to eat me? Was I nothing more than its next meal?*

It was a horrible thought, and I could only imagine what it would feel like if the blob chomped down on my arms, my legs....

Not now, Olivia, I told myself. *Don't think about that now. Just keep pedaling, focus on getting home safe. Getting in the house, calling Mom.*

The harder I pedaled, the faster I rode and the more distance I put between myself and the monster, the better I felt. I was also relieved the creature wasn't coming after me. When I glanced back, the blob appeared to be motionless, standing just off to the side of the road. When I reached our driveway and glanced back again, it was gone.

I sped up the driveway, hitting the brakes and

skidding to a stop near our front porch. I jumped off my bike and let it fall to the ground, not even taking the time to prop it up on the kickstand.

When I reached the porch, I turned around again.

No green blob monster.

But I *did* see something else.

Or, rather, someone else.

In the distance, on the shoulder of the road.

Someone on a bike, riding along the shoulder.

At first, nothing really added up. I often saw people ride their bikes on our road. There was a small group of cyclists who rode together on the weekends, and they would fly past our house like the wind, a tightly bound blur of aluminum and tires and muscle and sweat, heads down, their bodies curled like insects, legs pumping furiously.

This was not one of them.

This was—

"Max!" I shouted, even though I knew he was too far away to hear me. *"Max! Max! Look out!"*

I stood on the porch and waved my arms wide, up and down, signaling, hoping to catch his attention. Whether he could see me or not, I couldn't tell.

But in the ditch....

The green blob was climbing out! It was moving slowly, climbing the embankment toward the road, creeping along, ready for an ambush!

"Max!" I screamed again.

But by then, it was too late. Whether Max heard or saw me didn't matter.

The green blob burst from the ditch and attacked, knocking Max off his bicycle and onto the ground.

11

The next few seconds were like a dream, like things were moving in slow motion. I wasn't aware of time or how it passed; the only thing I was aware of was emotion. A terror exploded within me, a horror so great that it held me in its powerful grip and wouldn't let go.

Not far away, on the shoulder of the road, Max had been knocked from his bicycle. He rolled and turned, and when he saw what had caused his fall he leapt to his feet, picked up his bike, jumped on, and began pedaling as fast as he could.

"Hurry, Max!" I shouted. I don't know if he heard me or not, but I hoped he could. I hoped he knew I was there, that I had witnessed what had happened, that I was rooting for him.

The green blob was in pursuit, but it wasn't as fast as Max on his bicycle. The mass of dark jelly quickly gave up. It turned off the shoulder, ambled down the embankment, and vanished into the ditch.

Max, of course, saw none of this. He was focused forward, concentrating on pedaling, working as hard as he could to get away from the horrible green thing that had knocked him from his bike and sent him sprawling.

I jumped off the porch and began running. I met Max at the end of our drive. He was puffing and panting and out of breath.

"What...what...what hap...happened?" he gasped. "Wha...wha...what was that?"

I shook my head. "I don't know," I said. "But I saw it, too. It knocked you off your bike. Are you okay?"

Max nodded.

"Out of breath," he said, still gasping for air. He leaned forward on his handlebars. "But I'm all right."

I looked down the road, searching for the green attacker. I didn't see anything. No cars, no people, no horrible green blob. Nothing.

"That thing is dangerous," Max said.

"But what *is* it?" I asked.

"Some sort of green beast," Max said. "I didn't even see it coming. It knocked me off my bike, and the next thing I knew, I was eating gravel. I took one look at that—that *thing*—and got away as fast as I could."

"It chased me out of the woods just before you got here," I said.

Max looked at me, eyes wide, and I nodded and continued.

"It was in the woods, and—"

"What were you doing in the woods?" Max interrupted.

"I guess I was looking for it, sort of. I was curious about what happened to you yesterday. You know...with your foot and your shoe. I guess I just wanted to see if I could find anything. So I went back to look. That's when I saw branches move. I went into the woods and found that...thing...whatever it is...and it chased me. I was able to get on my bike and get away. That just happened, right before you got here."

"There's something really weird going on," I said.

"No kidding," Max said.

He was breathing a bit easier now. Sweat had formed on his forehead and face, creating a glossy sheen. The clouds had burned away, and the sunshine bore down upon us like hot, nuclear rays. It was going to be another humid, steamy day.

We stood there, baking in the sun, watching, and waiting. But we didn't see anything. No green blob, nothing moving. The view before us—the road, the ditch, the fields, and forest—was frozen. There was no breeze to play with the leaves on the trees, and nothing moved. It was eerie.

"I wonder where the thing went?" Max asked.

I shook my head. "I saw it go into the ditch while you were pedaling away" I replied.

"Let's go look for it," Max suddenly said.

My jaw fell, and I looked at him. "Are you out of your *mind?*"

Max shrugged. "Really, Olivia," he said. "We have bikes. We can move a lot faster than that thing."

I shook my head. "No," I said. "I don't think it's a good idea."

"It's probably just algae," Max said.

"Algae doesn't attack people," I insisted. "This

has got to be something else."

"Like what?" Max asked. "I mean...it's not like it's a bear or anything. I bet if we gave it a good kick the thing would probably pop like a balloon full of jelly. Come on."

Why? Why did I shake my head, get on my bike, and follow Max?

To this day, I don't know.

But I do know this:

It was a very, very bad idea.

12

"Wait," I said to Max. I still couldn't believe I'd agreed to go with him to look for the green blob.

"What?" Max asked.

"I'm going to get my phone," I said. "In case of an emergency."

"I don't think that'll happen," Max said. "Like I said: we have our bikes. We can get away."

"Just in case," I said.

After retrieving my phone from my room, I rejoined Max in the driveway. It was then that I noticed his tennis shoes.

"Your shoes look like they're too big for you," I said.

Max looked down. "That's because they're my brother's. I lost one of my shoes yesterday. It's the only pair of sneakers I had. My brother had an extra pair that he outgrew, but these are still a little too big."

Together, we rode our bikes along the shoulder of the road, keeping our heads up, our eyes open, ever vigilant and watching, looking for anything that moved. A truck passed by and honked its horn, but I didn't recognize the driver. It was probably someone who just honked to say 'hello.' But other than that, the day was quiet and calm.

We slowed as we approached the place where I'd watched the blob flee to the ditch.

"It was right about here," I said.

We slowed our bikes to a stop on the shoulder of the road. To our right, the embankment sloped down into a trough of gritty, dark, standing water. It was so thick and mud-choked that there was no way we could see deeper than the surface.

"That thing could be right there, hiding in the water, and we'd never know it," I said.

"Nah," Max said. "It would be moving around. We would see it."

Suddenly, a thought came back to me. Words

I'd spoken the day before were suddenly ringing in my head again.

It could never happen.

We had been talking about evil space algae attacking people, and Max said that it would make a great book. But I had said—

It could never happen.

I wasn't sure if I believed that anymore.

"See anything?" Max asked.

I shook my head. "Nope," I replied.

Max hopped off his bike and began pushing it along the shoulder, and I followed. Together, we took slow, deliberate steps, keeping our eyes on the drainage ditch and the dirty, brown water. Gravel crunched beneath our feet.

Finally, after we'd gone a distance, we stopped.

"I think we missed it," I said. "We've gone too far. That thing attacked you and went into the drainage ditch back there." I turned and pointed. "Let's go back and have another look."

Truthfully, I was hoping we wouldn't see anything. I didn't want to get a closer look at whatever it was. Yes, I was curious as to what the green blob could be, but I also felt a knot of danger, of warning, in the pit of my stomach. Something told me we'd be better off going to the park and playing or fishing. Or staying home and playing video games. Something...safe.

We followed the shoulder of the road, pushing our bikes along the edge of the embankment. There was no sign of anything unusual, nothing out of the ordinary, no weird tracks or anything like that. We passed the spot where the blob had caught Max's foot and taken his shoe, but there was nothing there.

Finally, Max stopped.

"That thing has to be here somewhere," he said.

"Maybe it's gone back to its spaceship," I snickered.

Max laughed. "You know," he said, "we *joke* about that...but it just might be true. Whatever it was that ate my shoe, well, that's not some sort of creature or animal that lives in the woods. Nothing *I've* ever heard of, anyway."

"Well, I don't see anything. Let's go back and—"

Max quickly raised his hand, stopping me in mid-sentence and silencing my words. He pointed down at the ditch.

Water was moving. There was something in the

ditch, something in the dirty grime, something just beneath the surface, causing a wake. If it were anywhere else, say, at the lake in the park, I would have said it was a fish.

But not here. Not in the drainage ditch. I knew for a fact there were no fish there.

So, that meant—

"I'm going to go check it out," Max said.

"I'm going to wait right here," I said.

"Chicken."

"Hey," I said, "someone needs to live to be a witness and call the police and tell them what happened." I was joking, of course, but I was also nervous. I didn't want Max to go down into the ditch alone...but I didn't want to go, either.

So, I waited while Max slowly made his way down the embankment toward the water...where he was about to come face to face with a monster.

13

"Be careful," I said. I was tense, and my hands gripped the handlebars of my bike as I watched Max. At the bottom of the ditch, the water was still moving in a small area, and Max was walking toward it. There was definitely something there, something just beneath the surface, causing the disturbance.

"Don't worry," Max said without looking up. "Man...it's a lot harder walking in shoes that are too big."

Max continued to move slowly, creeping toward the small body of water.

"See anything?" I called out.

Max shook his head. "Whatever it is, it's still

there," he replied.

Something broke the surface of the muddy water.

Max stopped.

I held my breath.

Then, Max turned and looked up at me from the bottom of the ditch. He wore an expression of surprise and shock. "It's a snapping turtle!" he said. "It's the biggest one I've ever seen!" He turned again to search the muddy water.

I exhaled, relieved. Snapping turtles are pretty common in Arkansas, and they live just about everywhere you find water. Some of them get really big, too. They look ferocious, with big heads and powerful jaws that hold on to their prey like a vise...so you want to keep your hands away from their head. But they're actually quite shy and harmless if you leave them alone. The smaller ones are kind of cute, and I've always thought it would be cool to have one as a pet, something I could keep in an aquarium in my bedroom. But my dad says no, that wild animals—including reptiles like snapping turtles—belong in the wild.

"This thing is gigantic!" Max said. He was

kneeling down now, crouching closer to the water. I could see the snapping turtle's head poking up from the surface, but the rest of his body was submerged and impossible to see in the silty, brown liquid.

"Don't fall in," I said. "You'll ruin your brother's shoes."

"He doesn't care," Max replied. "He can't wear them anymore, anyway."

"Okay," I said. "Now that we know what it is, let's go." I was still a little nervous and wary, and I glanced up and around to make sure I didn't see the green blob anywhere, hiding in the forest or maybe hunkered down in the grass. But I didn't see anything. Nothing out of the ordinary, anyway.

Max leaned closer to the water, and the snapping turtle decided that was too close. His head slipped beneath the surface, and he was gone.

Max stood. He turned and looked up at me.

"Man," he said. "By the size of that thing's head, he was probably as big as a laundry tub. I'll bet he weighs a ton!"

"Well, he's gone now," I said. "Let's go to my house and—"

Behind Max, the water churned and boiled. Max

was right: the snapping turtle must have been really big to create that size of a disturbance on the surface. There was a splash, and what suddenly broke the surface was, without question, not a snapping turtle.

It was big.

It was green.

It was inhuman.

And it was as big as Max.

14

The most shocking thing of all wasn't that the green blob had reappeared. What was incredible was the size of it! Less than an hour before, it had been much smaller, about the size of a beach ball. Now it was as big as Max, and twice as wide. Not only that, it now had more human-like features and qualities, including fat arms, legs, and a huge head with no neck. It had two dark eyes and what could only be a thin but wide mouth. Did it have a nose? I couldn't be sure. It was as though the creature had been crudely shaped with clay, like a little kid was trying to create a human but wasn't quite skilled enough. If the thing wasn't so scary-looking, I would say that it looked like a cartoon caricature.

But cartoons are usually funny. What I was seeing wasn't funny at all.

Max didn't move. He stood where he was in shoes too big for his feet, staring at the green monster staring at him. It was as though each were sizing up one another for a fight, trying to psych each other out. However, I couldn't see Max's face because his back was to me, and I was certain that his face was in the grip of a fear he'd never known before.

That grip was suddenly broken when the giant green blob moved. It wasn't a fast movement and it didn't lunge toward Max; rather, the beast sort of leaned over and forward.

This was all Max needed to free him of the spell he was under. He turned and ran, scaling the embankment with long strides. In seconds, he was at his bike.

But as for me? I couldn't take my eyes off the creature. I guess I was still trying to make sense of it, trying to figure out exactly what it was, what it was capable of. Where it came from.

An alien space blob, I kept thinking, recalling my conversation the day before with Max. Yes, it sounded like a science fiction book or movie, but there was no doubt that what I was seeing in the ditch was real and alive. It wasn't a creature from a book or a movie. The thing was as alive as I was.

As much as I wanted to flee, to pedal away on my bike as fast as my legs would pump, I couldn't. I was too mesmerized by the gargantuan green beast standing in the water in the ditch. Max, too, seemed unable to take his eyes away.

While we watched, the green blob picked up a large, basketball-sized rock from beneath the surface. With its meaty, fat arms, the motion was effortless. He held it out as though he was inspecting it, trying to figure out what it was.

Water dripped from the rock.

"What's it doing with that rock?" Max whispered.

"I don't know," I said. *"He doesn't seem to know what it is."*

"What if he throws it at us?" Max asked.

I paused. "I don't think he will," I replied. "He doesn't seem to know what it is."

"If he throws it at one of us," Max said, *"we're history. That thing has to weigh thirty pounds."*

Not far away, I saw the big turtle's head break

the surface, only for an instant before it vanished again. I was glad. I'd forgotten about the reptile, and I'm glad it had gotten far enough away from the green creature so it wouldn't get hurt.

But I was more worried about us.

"Let's get to my house," I said quietly, instinctively feeling my back pocket to make sure my phone was still there. *"When we know we're safe, I'll call Mom."*

In the ditch, the creature raised the rock. At first, I thought it was going to bring it down full force, dropping it into the water.

That's not what happened.

Instead, the green giant pulled it closer to his face. His mouth widened, and, while we watched, the beast ate the rock! He put the *entire thing* in his mouth! Not only that, the creature began to chew. We heard the rock breaking and crushing, like someone chewing cereal or potato chips...except this was a lot louder.

"Can you believe this?" Max hissed. *"Can you believe that thing just ate a rock?"*

I said nothing, but my answer would have been a solid 'no.' I couldn't believe what I was seeing and if anyone told me that they had seen something like this, I wouldn't believe them, either.

But I was seeing it with my own eyes. This wasn't some altered picture or video. This was reality, as real as reality gets, right here, right now.

A giant green blob was eating a huge rock and chewing it as if it were popcorn.

And if that wasn't strange enough?

Things got even weirder.

Suddenly, the green thing looked like it was going to be sick. Maybe he didn't like the taste of the rock, after all. I didn't know. But he opened his mouth and spit out the fragments, vomiting chunks of stone and green, bubbling saliva. The pieces of the rock fell, splashing into the water. Green slime dribbled down the creature's chin. It was the grossest thing I'd ever seen in my life.

Then, he suddenly looked up at us. I know it sounds crazy, but he looked...mad. He looked as though he'd been caught doing something embarrassing, and we were making fun of him. Which, of course, we weren't...but that didn't matter.

What mattered was that now the green beast was angry, and for whatever reason, he was angry with us.

That was when he lunged forward, with only one thing on his mind: to get to us.

15

"Let's get out of here!" Max wailed.

We took off on our bikes, and I pedaled as hard and fast as I could. Max was right by my side, so close that our bikes were almost touching. We raced along the shoulder, tires spitting gravel, putting distance between us and the rampaging green beast.

When I finally glanced back, the thing seemed to have given up. It had easily climbed to the top of the ditch, but by then we were already pedaling off. After a moment, it realized it wasn't going to be able to catch us. Turning, the thing lumbered back into the ditch and out of sight.

We pedaled without coasting until we reached

our driveway. I pulled my back brake lever and skidded to a stop. Max did the same, and we both turned and looked back up the road.

The green monster was gone. Oh, I knew he wasn't gone gone. He was still out there, somewhere in the ditch. But we couldn't see him at the moment.

I leaped from my bike and let it fall to the ground at the front porch. Max did the same, and he followed me as I hurried inside. As soon as I was in the living room, I pulled my phone from my back pocket and tapped Mom's number into the keypad. My call went straight to voicemail.

"Mom! There's a giant green monster here. It attacked me and Max. We're at home. We're okay, but that thing is out there somewhere. Call me back!"

I ended the call.

"Your Mom is never going to believe that," Max said.

"What?" I asked.

"You just told your mom that we were being attacked by a giant green monster," Max said. He grinned. "I know it's the truth and you know it's the truth, but your mom is going to think you've gone crazy."

Max was right. Now that I thought about it, my message did sound a bit crazy. Still, it was true, and Mom needed to know. After all, she could be in danger, too. What if that giant green thing attacked her car on her way home?

I swiped open the message app and sent a simple text to Mom: Call me.

"That's all we can do for now," I said. "Unless we call someone else. Do you want to call your mom?"

Max shook his head. "I don't think my Mom will believe me, either," Max said.

"How about the police?" I asked.

We looked out the living room window, at the front yard, the driveway, and the strip of road that faded into the distance. The sun was shining, and the day seemed perfect, like there was nothing at all wrong in the world.

But we knew different. Somewhere out there, hiding in the ditch or in the water, was that green beast.

"If we call the cops and they come and don't find anything, we're going to be in trouble," Max said. "People get in a lot of trouble when they call the police for no reason."

"But we have a reason," I replied. "We have a good reason."

"I know that and you know that," I replied. "But do they know that? Think about it, Olivia. What would you do if you were the police and some kid called you and said they were being attacked by a green monster from outer space?"

"We don't know if it's from outer space," I said.

"Then where did it come from? That...thing, whatever it is...is the exact color of that algae that was leaking from that canister yesterday when the truck flipped."

"But that's crazy," I said.

Max shrugged. "Crazier things have happened," Max replied. "Just because we don't know what's going on doesn't make it any less real."

I thought about that. Max was right. I thought about all the crazy things—legends, tall tales, folklore—that circulated among the population for years. Stories of bigfoot creatures, the Loch Ness monster, ghosts, flying saucers. No one had any proof of these things and many people laughed, thinking that the very idea of a monster living in the woods or a giant creature living in the water wasn't true. But just because they didn't have any evidence didn't mean that those beasts weren't real.

"So, then what?" I asked.

"I say we just wait for your mom to call you back," Max said. "Even if she doesn't believe your message, she'll call you back."

Suddenly, I remembered Mom's note and what she'd asked me to do. Despite everything that had happened, it now seemed really important. Without saying anything to Max, I hurried in to the kitchen. The slow cooker was on the counter, and I took the lid off. Mom's chili was cooking, and I was hit by a sudden blast of intense, spicy aroma.

I placed my phone on the dining room table, then picked up the big spoon from the counter and gave the goop a couple of stirs. Usually, you don't have to stir things that are in a slow cooker, but Mom just likes to 'move the goods around,' as she likes to say. Regardless, I was relieved that the chili seemed to be cooking just fine, and I had followed through on what Mom had asked.

I returned the lid to the cooker. Max was still in the living room, and he spoke.

"I still think it's weird that—"

Without warning, the sliding glass door—the one that opens to the back yard—exploded, sending fragments of shredded glass all over the kitchen.

16

The explosion of glass was so intense, so unexpected, that I nearly jumped out of my skin. It was as though an atomic bomb went off. First came the blast, the violent, powerful detonation...followed by a shockwave of showering glass.

I dropped the big spoon and turned.

It was one of...*them.*

A giant algae monster.

And I say 'them,' because this creature was obviously not the same creature that we spotted in the ditch, the one who'd ate the rock and pulverized it, turning it in to molten lava. It wasn't quite as big, either, standing a bit shorter than me.

But obviously, without question, it was just as deadly.

Max had heard the loud explosion and was now standing in the entryway of the kitchen, eyes wide, his face filled with horror.

"Go to my room!" I shouted.

We fled, rounding the corner into the hallway, and taking long strides to my bedroom door. I threw it open and rushed inside, spinning and grabbing Max, pulling him into the room and out of the way as I slammed the door closed.

"That...that thing...isn't the same one from the ditch!" I cried. "It's a different one! There's more than just one!"

"It's an invasion!" Max said. "An invasion of the algae creatures from outer space!"

Any other time, any other day, Max's words would have sounded ridiculous. They would have sounded like the rantings of a lunatic, a crazy person, someone who had lost touch with reality.

And yet, considering the circumstances, the gravity and seriousness of the situation, Max's words not only sounded rational and reasonable, they sounded perfectly normal. He was simply describing the facts of what was happening. And, at the moment, it really *did* seem like we were under attack from giant green space aliens.

I felt my heart pounding in my throat. Moments ago, I had been calmly stirring Mom's chili surprise. Now, my heart was racing and my blood was rushing through my veins. My thoughts were going a billion miles an hour, trying to think of what to do next.

"We have to call the police!" Max said. "We have to call the police *now!*"

Max was right. Even if Mom called me back and came rushing home, what would she do? She would be in danger, too...and I didn't want that to happen.

I reached into my back pocket to grab my phone, but before my hand even reached it, I realized my mistake.

My phone was on the dining room table, where I'd left it only moments ago.

Max noticed my look of horror. "What's the matter?" he asked.

"I left my phone on the table!" I replied.

"Nice going," he said.

"I didn't mean to!" I insisted. "How was I supposed to know that one of those things was going to break into the house like that?"

We heard shuffling sounds in the kitchen.

"He's in your house!" Max said.

I tiptoed to my bedroom door. Stopped. Listened.

I heard glass crunching on the linoleum floor.

I grasped the brass doorknob. Very slowly, being careful not to make a sound, I turned it, pulling the door open just a crack, just enough to see down the hallway.

I couldn't make out much, but I could see a portion of the green creature in the kitchen. At the moment, he didn't appear to be moving.

"What's it doing?" Max asked.

"Just standing there, I think," I replied quietly. "It doesn't look like he's doing anything."

"We have to get your phone," Max said. "That's our lifeline. Your mom is the only one who knows we're in trouble, and I doubt she even believes the message you left her."

Max was right, of course. We needed to call for help. The police could be here in minutes, but only if we called them. They can't respond to an emergency if they don't know about it.

So, we waited. Max leaned forward, peering over my shoulder, so he, too could see what was going on in the kitchen.

"What's it doing now?" he whispered.

"Still nothing," I replied. "It's just standing there."

After what seemed like forever, we finally saw the beast move. In the kitchen, we heard glass crunching.

Then, we heard no sounds at all.

Did we dare?

I opened the door a bit more, trying to see into the kitchen. My scope of vision was limited, but I could see my phone sitting on the dining room table, where I left it.

But I didn't see the creature. I was certain that the green goblin had gone outside.

"Wait here," I whispered to Max.

"Is he gone?" Max whispered back.

"I hope so," I said. *"I've got to get my phone. It's our only hope."*

Slowly, quietly, I pulled the door open.

"Be super careful," Max said.

"I will," I replied.

And I was. I was very careful. I moved slowly and quietly, like a cat in the shadows.

But being careful wasn't enough. I was walking directly into a trap.

I just didn't know it yet.

17

I took slow, cautious steps down the hall, careful to place my shoe heel-first to the floor, ever so softly, slowly. When I reached the kitchen, I cautiously peered around the wall.

The scene was a disaster. There was glass everywhere: the floor, the counter, the dining room table. Mom was going to freak out when she saw the chaos and destruction.

But I couldn't worry about Mom's reaction at the moment. I needed to call for help, I needed to contact the police or maybe the National Guard. And in order to do that, I needed my phone...which was on the dining room table, in the exact place I left it.

It was a relief to see it there, and I wanted to rush out and grab it. But I didn't. From where I stood, I could see outside through the doorway that used to be a pane of heavy glass...but I knew that horrible green germ could be nearby. I didn't see him at the moment. Which meant that if I was very quiet and moved slowly....

I took a single step into the kitchen, allowing my weight to slowly shift to my right foot. I had to step on shards of broken glass, as there was no way around it. The sharp pieces crunched like gravel as the heel of my shoe pressed down.

Then, I lifted my other foot and held it in the air for a moment. I looked around and outside for any sign of movement. Nothing.

I turned my head and looked back. Max was in the doorway, eyes wide as he watched. He gave me the 'thumbs up' sign, and I returned the gesture.

Slowly, I lowered my foot to the floor. The broken glass under my shoe crunched and cried out.

Almost there—

I heard a noise in the stairwell. On the other side of the kitchen is a narrow entry that leads out to our garage. There are six steps that go down to a landing and a door. The landing is usually packed with shoes, boots, and a couple of raincoats and umbrellas. If it's raining, Mom wants me to come in through the garage and take my shoes off so I don't track mud all over the house.

But at the moment, muddy shoes and rain were the last thing I was worried about. No, I was more worried about what had made that soft noise I'd heard.

I managed a quick glance behind me. Max was still in the doorway, watching and waiting.

I turned back around, just as I heard the noise again. A scraping sound, the same sound my shoe made as it fell upon the broken glass.

My phone was only a few feet away.

I'll run and grab it, I thought. *I'm fast. I can grab it and run back to my room.*

In the stairwell I saw a movement of green, and that changed my plans. Not only that, I saw movement outside, beyond the empty pane of the sliding glass door.

Not waiting to see anymore and put myself at further risk, I quickly spun and made a mad dash down the hallway, leaving my phone on the table. When I reached my room, Max stepped out of the way and I darted inside, closing the door behind me.

"What happened?" Max asked. "Why didn't you get your phone?"

"There are two of those things out there!" I said. "There's one in the stairwell by the door that goes to the garage and another one outside. It's like they're multiplying on their own!"

"Sort of like a virus," Max said.

As crazy as it sounded, that made a lot of sense. What if that's what those green things were? Giant viruses of some sort? Cells that split and reproduce on their own?

It was a scary thought, and I wondered what that would mean. I wondered what they were capable of. After all, we'd already watched one of them eat a rock. They were obviously very powerful. I hated to think of what would happen to Max or me if we were unfortunate enough to fall into one of their giant, fat hands.

"Well, don't look now," Max said, gazing out my bedroom window. "But there's more trouble."

I looked out the window. In the distance, I could see a car coming on the highway.

In the drainage ditch, I saw a giant green

blob-monster paused on the slope, as if he were waiting for just the right moment.

The driver of the car wouldn't be able to see the creature, and would have no idea what was waiting for him.

It was going to be an ambush.

18

Max and I walked to my bedroom window, pressing our noses against the glass.

"We've got to do something," Max said.

"What?" I asked. "There's nothing we can do. The driver of the car is too far away to see us. Besides: even if he saw us, all he would see is two kids waving their arms like crazy. He wouldn't know what we meant."

The car continued. From where we were, it appeared the vehicle was coming directly at us, but that was because of the direction of the road. The highway curved a little before it reached our house, so the car would follow it and veer to our right as it passed.

But it didn't look like it was going to make it that far. Not if that freaky green blob of algae had anything to do with it.

"It's like that thing is stalking the car," Max said. "It's like it knows it's coming and is waiting for it."

The car was still some distance away, looming larger and larger as it continued toward us.

"I wish you had a bottle rocket or something," Max said.

I looked at him. "What good would a bottle rocket do?"

"Well, we could light it off and shoot it at the car."

"And what would *that* do?" I asked.

Max shrugged, bewildered. "I dunno. Maybe alert the driver to something wrong."

"Yeah," I said. "It would alert the driver that there were kids shooting bottle rockets at him. That would only make him mad."

"Maybe we could shoot the bottle rockets at the green monster," Max said.

"Look at that thing," I said, nodding. "I don't think a bottle rocket is going to have any effect on him.

We need one of those guided missiles they have in the military."

"That would be cool," Max said. "That would blow that thing sky high."

"And green goop would be everywhere," I said.

The car was getting closer to the green blob.

"It's moving," I said.

The green algae monster, as big as it was, appeared to be hunkering down close to the embankment. It was the perfect color, too, as he appeared nearly invisible in his surroundings of tall, uncut grass. The thing reminded me of a grizzly bear, only this creature was green and didn't have claws. Still, I had a feeling it was every bit as deadly as a grizzly.

"Man, that guy in the car isn't going to stand a chance," Max said.

And it was a guy, too, as we could now see. A single, male driver was behind the wheel, completely oblivious to the waiting creature hiding in the ditch. Of course, I had no idea who was behind the wheel...but I still was afraid for him. I didn't want to see anyone get hurt. Anyone. I think most people feel that way. When we see someone in danger, we want to warn them, want to help them. Maybe that's because we all know what it's like to be afraid, we all know what it's like to feel hurt, and if we have a chance to help others, we would do it. *I* would, anyway.

But this was different. If we went running from my bedroom and outside, there was no doubt we would be putting us in just as much danger as the driver of the car. And it might not help, anyway. It was a horrible, helpless feeling.

"I'm not sure if I want to see this," I said.

"But maybe the green thing won't do anything," Max said. "And even if he does, I think the car is a lot faster than he is."

"Yeah," I agreed. "But deer are probably a lot faster, and cars hit them all the time. And this thing, whatever it is, is a lot bigger than a deer. If that guy hits it with a car, who knows what will happen?"

"I think we're about to find out," Max said.

The green beast, looming large but crouching low, appeared to be readying for an attack. It was now just off the shoulder of the road. From where we were, it looked exactly like a big, green bush. That's all. A harmless plant, growing just off the side of the road.

The car approached.

The green, hideous monster attacked.

19

Watching the events unfold through my bedroom window gave the event a bizarre, movie-like appearance, as though we were watching what was happening on a big screen. But there certainly no denying that what we were seeing wasn't some trick of light in a movie theater. It was real, and it was happening now.

The giant green monster rose from the ditch. In the next instant it was on the shoulder, and then it placed itself directly into the path of the oncoming car.

Max gasped. I held my breath.

The car swerved violently to the other side of the highway. If another car had been coming in the opposite direction, they would have hit head-on.

Miraculously, however, the car missed the green monster! I don't think the driver had time to hit the brakes, and turning the wheel and swerving was his only option. The car lurched sideways, narrowly missing the green giant in its path.

The monster turned, raising its fat arms in frustration as the car sped on. It was traveling much faster now, and I could see the driver looking up into his rearview mirror, no doubt wondering what had just happened, what he'd just seen on the highway. He probably didn't believe it himself.

And behind him, still standing on the road, was the green monster. From where I stood in my room, the creature looked like a giant, lime-colored potato. With arms and legs and a head, of course.

"I can't believe that just happened!" Max said. "I can't believe that guy missed the monster! Did you see how close he came?"

I nodded. "Oh, I saw it, all right," I said. "I don't believe it, either, but it happened. That driver is probably the luckiest guy in the world."

"I was sure he was going to hit that thing," Max said.

While we watched, the car sped past. We caught a quick glimpse of the horrified driver as he flew down the highway. Suddenly, I had a completely different thought, and I laughed out loud.

Max frowned. "What's so funny?" he asked.

"I just thought about how silly it's going to sound when he tries to explain to someone what just happened," I said. "Imagine that guy going home to tell his wife that he almost hit a giant green vegetable with his car!"

"No one will believe him," Max said.

"No way," I said.

Farther down the road, the green monster moved to the shoulder, then slipped into the ditch. He vanished from our sight, and I figured that maybe he was simply hiding, hunkering down by the water.

I heard a noise in the kitchen, and that brought me back to our own predicament, our own problems we were facing. There were green monsters around our house—inside our house, too—and we were in as much danger as the driver of the car had been. The only difference is that we didn't have a vehicle to escape in. We were trapped in my bedroom, at least for the time being. Our only lifeline, our only way out, our only way of escape was to use my phone to call for help. And, my phone was still on the dining room table. I know it was as close as the other room, but at that moment it felt like it was miles away.

"What now?" Max asked.

"The way I see it," I replied, "there's only one way out of this. We've got to get my phone and call for help."

"What if we just wait?" Max replied. "Sooner or later, your mom is going to come home."

"That's what I'm afraid of," I said. "She has no way of knowing what's been going on here. She has no idea of the danger we're in, or the danger she'll be in. Even if she makes it past the monster out there in the ditch, there are still the ones here, around our house. You and I have been pretty lucky. I don't think Mom will be so fortunate."

"We could try our bikes," Max said.

I thought about this for a moment. It didn't seem like a bad idea, as I was sure we could pedal faster than the green beasts. But even if we were able to get away, even if we were able to go for help, there was still a chance Mom could come home in the meantime.

"No," I said. "I don't think that's a good idea. We have to get my phone and call for help. The sooner, the better."

I tiptoed to the bedroom door, grasped the knob, turned it, and pulled. Carefully, I peeked through the small opening. I could only see a portion of the kitchen, but enough to see the broken glass all over the floor...and one of the green monsters standing near the dining room table, blocking my view of the phone.

Max crept up next to me. *"See anything?"* he whispered.

I nodded without saying anything, never taking my eyes off the beast. And that's when it did something so unexpected, so incredible, all I could do was hold my breath and watch.

"We are in big, big trouble," Max whispered.

20

The creature was changing right before our very eyes.

Now, when I say 'changing,' I don't mean it was becoming some sort of other creature. It wasn't like that at all. No, what I mean is that its shape was slowly shifting, becoming more blob-like. For one hopeful moment, I thought it was melting and dying, right there in the kitchen. But I knew it was too much to hope for.

"What's it doing?" Max asked. *"What's going on?"*

I shook my head. *"I don't know,"* I whispered back. *"It looks like it's changing into something."*

"Like a caterpillar changes into a butterfly?" Max

asked.

That alone was a horrifying thought. As crazy as it sounded, what if that were to happen? We had no idea what the thing was, what it was really capable of doing. What if Max was right? What if the thing sprouted wings, and was able to fly?

The nightmarish vision quickly spun out of control. In my mind, I could see dozens—even hundreds—of giant, flying green monsters descending upon our little town. Men, women, and children, running away in terror, screaming. People being scooped up and carried away by the green beasts. It was like envisioning the end of the world, and it all had started in my hometown of Russellville, Arkansas.

I flung the horrifying vision from my mind, as it was only freaking me out more than I already was. Besides: what was happening in the kitchen, in real life, was every bit as strange, every bit as terrifying.

The creature was splitting in two.

While we watched, the thing squirmed and wriggled until it looked like a giant blog of gelatin. Then, we began to see arms re-form. And legs. And two heads.

"It's copying itself!" Max hissed.

Like a giant virus, I thought. *It's like a big, huge virus, splitting itself into two separate life forms.*

Which, of course, gave me another nightmarish vision: what if that's what these things were? What if they were a virus and could infect the human race? I'd read about diseases throughout history that wiped out millions of people. In school, our class studied the Black Plague, which occurred during the Middle Ages. In just four years, the disease was responsible for wiping out up to 200 million people! Then, the Spanish flu of 1918 infected up to 500 million people, and up to 100 million of those didn't survive.

Even today, diseases like that were making the news, and scientists and doctors said it might only be a matter of time before another pandemic strikes.

What if that's what was happening now? What if Max and I were watching the birth of a new pandemic, a horrifying new disease of giant viruses infecting mankind?

And somehow, I knew that the space algae had something to do with it. I knew that the spilled canister we'd spotted the day before, with the experimental algae that had been sent into space, had to be connected with these creatures. I know it wasn't anyone's fault, but that wasn't important at the moment. The most important thing, right now, was getting my phone and calling for help. And we would have to do it without coming into contact or being attacked by those giant green gremlins.

"Now there are two of them," Max said.

We watched as one of the green beasts, now fully formed, began to move. It stretched its fat arms and turned its chubby head as if waking up from a nap. Then, it shuffled across the glass-strewn floor and out the doorway where the sliding glass door had once been.

The other green blob appeared to be facing the other way. It was standing near the cupboards, next to the slow cooker on the counter.

I've got to stir Mom's chili, I suddenly thought, and I nearly laughed out loud. It was silly to think about that when there were much more important things to think about.

Without saying anything, Max pulled the door open and slipped past me. He turned quickly and put a finger to his lips.

"Wait here," he whispered. *"I'm going to sneak up behind that thing and get your phone."*

I didn't have time to tell him it was a bad idea. I didn't have time to convince him that it was a poor choice. I didn't have time to tell him that things could go wrong really, really fast.

Before I knew it, Max was tiptoeing toward the kitchen...where he was about to find out, on his own, what a terrible decision he had made.

21

I couldn't stop Max. I couldn't say anything, because I didn't want to make any noise that might alert the green monster as to where we were.

But when Max turned to look at me, I tried to speak with him with my eyes. I glared at him, pleading, warning, urging...all of this I tried to convey to him in my wide-eyed stare.

I think, by the way he looked at me, he knew that what he was attempting was dangerous and foolish. On one hand, I thought his decision was probably the worst thing he could have done.

But, then again, it was also very brave. He was risking his life to get to the phone and call for help, to save our lives. Not only our lives, but to save the lives of others. It was possible that the driver of the car had already called the police, but would they believe him? I tried to imagine the conversation between the man and the emergency dispatcher.

Um, hello...yes, I'd like to report an attack. Yes. I was in my car, driving along, when I was attacked by a giant green booger. Yes, that's right. A giant green booger. He came out of the ditch and attacked my car and....

I was pretty sure they would laugh at him and then hang up.

But if Max was able to get to the phone, we could call for help, too. When the police received another call about the same thing—a huge, green monster—they might decide to investigate.

Max was risking his life. For us, and for others.

He looked at me, smiled, and gave me the 'thumbs up' signal. I mouthed the words *be careful,* and he turned and continued moving toward the kitchen. He crept along the wall, slowly, stepping cautiously.

In the kitchen, the single, green blob remained. From what I could see, it looked like the creature was facing the other way...at least for the time being.

And I thought about what had just happened when we'd watched the thing split into two. What if that happened again? Two would become four, four would become eight, eight would become sixteen....

There will be thousands of them—hundreds of thousands of them—in no time at all, I thought. Their number will quickly become enormous, and they'll be out of control.

And while I wasn't quite sure what they were capable of, what threat they posed, or what they wanted, I was certain it wasn't good.

Max reached the kitchen. He peered around the corner. At this point, he was only a few feet away from my phone. He would have to take three steps across the glass-covered tile floor, grab the phone, and get away.

And he would have to do it without being noticed.

He took one step, slowly putting his foot down. He had to be careful not to step hard and make the glass crunch beneath the sole of his shoe.

One step....

So far, so good. He was in full view of the monster now, and if the creature turned around, Max would be directly in front of him.

Two steps....

He paused and leaned forward, reaching for the phone, reaching as though his arms would grow and he would be able to grab it....

But no. He would need to take one more step in order to grab the phone.

He turned. Looked at me. Our eyes met, only for a moment. Then he looked back at the phone.

Reaching....

He raised his foot, slowly moving it up, out, forward, down, down, slowly, slowly....

His foot touched the floor. Quietly. He didn't make a sound. That alone was heroic.

But he wasn't done. He hadn't achieved what he'd set out to do. He still needed to get my phone.

Max leaned forward, reaching. Stretching, reaching....

The creature remained motionless. At any moment it could turn, and Max would be a goner. Again, I remembered what had happened to that huge rock when the creature ate it. I didn't want to think about what would happen if it got hold of Max.

The phone was just out of Max's reach, inches

from his fingers. He stretched more, leaning, leaning—

Whether he was off balance or what, I don't know, but suddenly, one foot slipped out from beneath him. Both arms went up and out. He tried to grasp at something, anything, that might keep him from falling.

There was nothing for him to grab, nothing to break his fall.

I screamed as Max went down, slamming to the kitchen floor, flat on his back.

The horrible green beast spun.

It was all over for my friend.

22

Despite my initial shock, despite my scream of surprise and horror, I sprang into action without even thinking. In three steps, I was down the hall and at the entryway of the kitchen. Max was still on the floor, gasping for breath, as the fall had knocked the wind from his lungs. He was helpless, at least for the moment.

The green creature, surprised, was staring at us. This was my very first close look at one of the things, and it was more hideous than I had thought.

For starters, the thing appeared to have no skeletal structure at all—it was just a mass of green jelly. It had fat arms and legs and a wide, bulbous head. Tiny, pinprick eyes and a wide mouth without lips. Without any doubt, it was far uglier than anything I'd seen on television or in the movies.

"Max!" I shouted. "Get up!"

Max was still struggling to get his breath, and I had to do something. I knew it would only be seconds before the green beast took action of his own, and I couldn't let that happen.

Reaching over Max, I grabbed one of the dining room chairs. I picked it up and swung it, heaving it at the creature as hard as I could. Then, without waiting to see what effect it had, I knelt down and grabbed one of Max's hands.

"You've got to stand!" I shouted. "Get up! Watch out for the glass!"

Somehow, Max made it to his knees. From there, I jerked him to his feet and pulled, mostly dragging him down the hall and to my bedroom. I slammed the door behind us as Max fell to the floor, doubling up, gasping for air.

I bent down on one knee.

"Are you okay?" I asked. Sure, it was a silly question, but what else was I going to ask?

Max nodded and tried to respond, but all he could do was spit out parts of a word.

"Okay," I said. "Don't try to speak. Catch your breath. I think we're safe...unless that thing tries to break the door down."

While Max recovered on the floor, I moved toward my bedroom door. Carefully, I opened it a thin crack and peered out through the slice with one eye.

In the kitchen, the green blob was eating the chair! The chair was made mostly of metal, but the monster was bending the legs without effort and cramming the pieces into his mouth. It made a horrible crunching sound, like bones, and I cringed. I couldn't imagine what would happen if that thing got hold of one of us.

And on the table?

My phone.

Max had been so, so close, but so very far.

I closed the door and went to him, kneeling down.

"I...I'm okay," he said, before I had a chance to say anything. "I...I almost had your...your phone."

"I know," I said.

"I'm sorry," said Max.

I shook my head. "Don't be. You were braver than I would have been. Besides, you couldn't know

129

you were going to slip and fall on the glass. Are you cut?"

Max rolled to his side and into a kneeling position. "I don't think so," he said.

"You're lucky." I grabbed one of his arms. "Can you stand?"

Still holding his arm, I stood. Max stood with me. He was fine, other than the fact that he looked shaken and a bit winded.

"That thing ate the chair," I said.

"We are going to have a lot more to worry about if we don't do something," Max said. "We can't stay in your bedroom forever. That thing knows we're here."

"Maybe not," I said hopefully. "We don't know how smart they are."

"We know they're smart enough to plan an ambush," Max said. "They have some sort of intelligence."

"But we're smarter," I said. Obviously, I had no way of knowing this. I was just trying to stay positive, to be hopeful.

"Well, for now," Max said, turning to look out my bedroom window, "for now, we're just going to have to—"

Max's sentence was cut short, and his body tensed. His arm shot out, pointing.

"Is that who I think it is?"

I looked out the window, expecting to see a police car or some other emergency vehicle.

Nope.

I gasped, suddenly remembering the phone call I'd received earlier in the day. I'd forgotten all about it...until now.

JoJo.

She was on her bicycle, pedaling along the shoulder of the road.

She had said she was going to ride over later in the day.

It was now later in the day.

JoJo was coming.

And she had no idea of the horror waiting for her in the drainage ditch.

23

I have never felt so helpless in my life.

Max and I stood in my bedroom, staring out the window, watching JoJo in the distance. She was pedaling smoothly, not in a hurry, taking her time. Even from afar, we could see her pink bike helmet glistening in the sun like a neon insect.

And in the ditch—

Even before either one of us could speak, it was too late. We saw the green beast rise from the ditch and begin climbing the slope toward the highway.

Toward JoJo.

And then, incredibly, JoJo stopped pedaling and began to coast. She, too, had spotted the beast, but instead of fleeing, she'd done the exact opposite.

She stopped. Stared. She sat on her bike, looking at the huge green thing coming toward her.

"What's she doing?" Max said, bewildered. "Why did she stop? Why isn't she trying to get away?"

"She probably doesn't realize what it is," I said. "She's probably in shock."

JoJo's shock didn't last long. Suddenly, realizing the potential danger she was in, her thin legs turned into churning windmills. As the green monster crested the rise of the slope and reached the shoulder, JoJo took off on her bike, quickly putting distance between her and the green blob.

But the green monster didn't retreat like it had after it had attacked the car. This time, the creature attacked. It was after JoJo. Yes, the beast wasn't as fast as she was on her bike, but he was still pursuing her. JoJo was leading the horrible monster right to our house.

Toward us.

Still, JoJo had no other choice. Somehow, we had to help her. We had to get her into my bedroom. We might not be safe for very long, but for the time being, it was our only hope.

I raced to the window and slid it open, then I opened the screen. From outside our house, the window was shoulder-height, but if Max and I worked together, we could pull her through.

"What are you doing?!?!" Max hissed. We still needed to be quiet, mindful of the creature that was still in the kitchen.

"We've got to get her in here," I said. "If she goes through the front door, she's going to be eaten alive by that green thing in the kitchen!"

That made sense to Max.

"We just need to get her attention so she knows," I said. "Wave to her so she sees us!"

Max and I leaned out the window and began flailing our arms. We didn't shout or say anything, not wanting our voices to draw more attention.

JoJo was whipping along the shoulder of the road, hair trailing from behind her, pink helmet glowing and bobbing in the sun.

And behind her—

"Is it just me, or is that thing moving faster?" Max asked.

"I think it's moving faster," I replied. "I hope JoJo makes it."

"I think she will," Max said.

We continued waving, and JoJo saw us. She continued pedaling, legs pumping, until she reached our front lawn. She rode up to the house and dove from her bike. It tumbled to the grass and came to a rest on its side, its rear wheel spinning.

The green beast that had been chasing her was some distance away, but it was still coming.

"Give us your hands!" I said.

JoJo raised both hands. Max and I each took one, and we pulled. JoJo pulled. We struggled for a moment, leaning, pulling back, using all our strength and all our weight. When JoJo was halfway through the window I let go of her hand and wrapped both of my arms around her waist. I pulled and nearly fell backward, but Max caught me at the last moment and prevented JoJo and me from tumbling to the floor.

JoJo's eyes were huge, but before she could speak, I raised a finger to my lips, indicating for her to be silent. I leaned closer to her and whispered everything that had happened, everything we knew. Which, of course, wasn't a lot. She listened in disbelief as we told her about the creatures, including the one currently in the kitchen, how we'd seen them eat a rock and a chair. I told her about the truck rollover the day before and how we thought it had a lot to do with what was going on.

"So...these things are like...algae monsters?" JoJo asked.

"We think so," Max replied.

"My phone is in the kitchen," I said. "We have to get it so we can call for help."

"Then let's do it," JoJo said.

"We already tried once," Max said.

"Yeah, well, I'm here now," JoJo said defiantly. "And I'm not going to sit here and wait for some giant green goober to eat all three of us. I'm going to come up with a plan."

And she did.

24

"How many of those things are there?" JoJo asked.

Max and I shrugged as we glanced at each other. "We don't know," I said.

"We watched one of them split into two," Max said. "So that means there could be a bunch more already."

"How many have you seen?" JoJo asked.

Again, I glanced at Max. "I'm not sure," I said. "Maybe four or five."

"But those might have already split in two, so there might be double that," Max said.

JoJo walked to the bedroom door and opened it a crack. She leaned close to it and cautiously peered down the hall and into the kitchen. Then she drew back.

"It looks like there's just the one in the kitchen," she said. "That's good. So, let's do this before it splits in two."

"Do *what?*" Max asked.

"Go and get that phone," JoJo said. "We don't have any other choice. We have to get Olivia's phone and call for help. We can't just wait here and hope for help to arrive. We might get eaten alive by that time."

"I don't want to be eaten alive," Max said. "My parents would be mad, and they would miss me."

"They would *replace* you," JoJo said with a playful smirk.

Max shrugged.

"So, how do we do it?" I asked. "Max already tried to sneak into the kitchen. That thing almost got him."

"Instead of sneaking into the kitchen," JoJo said, "we go in and get the monster's attention. We get him to chase one of us."

"What?!?!" I said.

"Let me finish," JoJo said. "We get the thing to follow one of us into the living room. Once we draw him out of the kitchen, one of us can grab the phone and run back to the bedroom with it."

"But what if that thing splits in two?" Max asked.

"That's why we've got to hurry," JoJo replied.

"One thing," I said. "What happens to the person who distracts the monster? Where do they go?"

"Out the front door, around the front of the house, and to your bedroom window," JoJo said. "So, it will work like this: Max...you're going to create the diversion. You'll go first. Just stand by the kitchen and get the attention of the creature. When he comes after you, let him follow you to the front door."

"Easy for you to say," Max said.

"I don't think it'll be that hard," JoJo said. "If these things aren't very intelligent—and they don't seem to be—it shouldn't be that difficult to outsmart them."

"And what about me?" I asked. "Do I get my phone?"

JoJo nodded. "As soon as the monster is out of the kitchen and following Max, you run into the kitchen, grab your phone, and run back to your room. It shouldn't take you more than five seconds.

Meanwhile, when Max makes it to your bedroom window, I'll start to pull him in. And as soon as you get back from the kitchen, you'll have to help me. I won't be able to pull Max through the window by myself."

"Sounds pretty risky," Max said.

"Everything in life is risky," JoJo said.

"I wish I was as confident about this as you are," I said.

"Well, we have to do something," JoJo said. "I'm not just going to sit here in your bedroom and wait for something to happen. If we do that, there's no telling what those things will do. And like I said, we have no idea when help is going to arrive. Or if it ever will. We've got to get that phone and call the police. It's our only hope."

"JoJo is right," Max said.

I knew she was, too. And now that there were three of us, JoJo's plan seemed workable. But we would have to act fast.

"Let's go," I said.

"Wait," said Max.

JoJo and I looked at him.

"What...um," he stammered. "What if...if that thing catches me before you guys can pull me through the bedroom window?"

"I wouldn't worry," JoJo said. "You probably taste terrible. One small bite and that thing will probably drop you and have to go wash his mouth out."

"Ha ha ha," Max sneered. "Funny. You're not the one that's going to be chased by one of those things."

"I think it's a good plan," I said, trying to sound reassuring. "With the three of us, we can do it. We'll have a better chance with all of us working together."

"This will work," JoJo said.

But as the saying goes: nothing ever goes as planned. That's why people always create a backup plan, a 'plan B.'

We didn't have a 'plan B.' If something went wrong, we didn't have a backup plan.

But it won't go wrong, I thought. Hoped.

Unfortunately, hoping wasn't going to help us succeed. Hoping was simply about thinking positive, acting positive, working toward the best solution.

And, in the end, my hope didn't matter. All the hope in the world wasn't going to stop things from making a bad situation even *worse.*

25

"Okay," JoJo said. "Let's hurry up and get this done."

That's one thing about JoJo that I've always liked. She always got down to business. When she wants to get something done, she does it. No messing around. At school one day, one of our assignments was to write an essay about what we wanted to be when we grow up. JoJo's essay was called *Why I will be President of the United States*. She read it out loud from the front of the room and when she finished, she looked up and asked "Okay...who's voting for me?" Everyone in class raised their hand. Even our teacher, Ms. Figbee, raised her hand. The funny thing was, nobody really doubted that JoJo would run for

President. There's a law that says you had to be at least thirty-five years old, but JoJo said she might be ready before that and would work to change the law. She wasn't kidding, and we all knew it.

Max, standing by my bedroom door, looked nervous. I would be, too, if I were in his shoes. His job was dangerous, as he was the one who would have to get the attention of the green monster. Not only that, for our plan to work, the thing would have to chase him.

JoJo sensed Max's apprehension. "Don't worry," she said. "This will work. I promise." She looked at me. "Are you ready, Olivia? You're going to have to grab your phone and get back here right away to help me get Max through your window."

I still wasn't sure if our plan was going to work, but I knew that JoJo was right. It really was our only option. Besides…we couldn't just wait for help to arrive if no one knew we were in trouble. And I was sure that when Mom listened to my phone message, she would just laugh and think I was kidding.

"All right," I said. "Let's get this done."

Max slowly opened the bedroom door. JoJo and I waited, watching him creep the short distance down the hall. When he was almost to the kitchen, he stopped and looked back at us. JoJo threw him the 'thumbs up' sign and nodded.

Max poked his head around the corner and peered into the kitchen. Then, taking a deep breath, he stepped out of the hall and stood where the kitchen and the living room intersected.

"Hey!" he said, waving his arms in the air. "Hey, you ugly pile of jelly! Come get me!"

It worked. We heard a noise from the kitchen, and Max suddenly spun and fled into the living room...followed by the green monster!

"He's coming after me!" Max shouted. We couldn't see him, but we heard loud footsteps as he bounded through the living room. The front door crashed open.

"Go! Go! Go!" JoJo shrieked in my ear.

I sprang, darting down the hall and into the kitchen—

I stopped abruptly, and the glass beneath my shoes caused my feet to slide on the tile.

Coming through the sliding glass door was another green beast!

He looked at me.

I looked at him.

The phone was on the table.

Did I dare try to grab it? Could I snap it up and still manage to get away?

Yes. Yes, I had to. There was no other option. I simply had to succeed. I had to get the phone. It was our lifeline, our only hope.

I gathered all my courage and was about to lunge forward and grab the phone—

Too late.

The green beast beat me to it. He reached out with his gigantic, fat arm, and scooped up my phone. In one single, terrible motion, he popped my phone into his mouth and began to chew.

Horrified, I could only stare. That was it. My phone, our only way of calling for help, was gone. I had failed. Not only that, I was now face-to-face with one of the most horrible, horrifying, ugly things I'd ever seen in my life. He had no right to eat my phone. He had no right to threaten us. We hadn't done anything wrong. We hadn't done anything to hurt those things.

And that's when I got mad.

26

From where I stood in the kitchen, I could hear Max and JoJo struggling in my bedroom. Max had made it to my window, and, from the sounds of it, JoJo was struggling to pull him through.

This was chaos. This was madness. We hadn't caused this. We hadn't done anything to deserve this. My friends and I had been thrown into this mess through no fault of our own. We hadn't done a thing…we were three innocent kids caught up in a horrifying, science fiction nightmare.

I was boiling mad. Instead of running away, instead of trying to flee, I turned to look for something, anything I could use as a weapon. In the drawer, we had a bunch of kitchen knives, but I didn't think they would do much.

But on the counter, in the slow cooker....

I took one giant step and reached out. The chili ladle was on the counter, next to the slow cooker. I snapped it up with my right hand. With my left, I grabbed the heavy, plastic lid of the pressure cooker and tossed it aside.

The giant algae monster came at me.

I dipped the ladle into the chili and filled the scoop. Then I spun, aimed as best as I could, and threw the hot liquid into the face of the attacking green behemoth.

I'm not sure exactly what I'd expected to happen. I hoped that, because the liquid was hot, it would slow the beast, causing it pain, causing it to retreat. Maybe once it knew that we were going to fight back, that it wasn't going to be so easy to overtake us, it would leave us alone.

But what happened next was completely unexpected.

When the chili came in contact with the beast's flesh—if that's what you could call it—the beast stopped in its tracks. The chili hitting the creature's face began to sizzle, making crackling, sparking sounds. The liquid instantly began eating away at the green gel. Steamy smoke rose up, twirling and swirling. The beast's body began to shake. It waved its arms and moved its legs as though it was trying to get away, but by then, the chili had disintegrated most of the creature's head. Brown smoke continued to rise, and the crackling sounds lingered. In seconds the beast had collapsed, leaving only a giant mound of puddled goop on the kitchen floor.

I was stunned. I looked at the mass of smoldering green jelly on the floor. I looked at the ladle in my hand. Chili was dripping from it, and droplets were landing in the green goo. The liquid had the effect of acid, causing the goop to burn with every drop of Mom's chili.

A scream came from my bedroom.

"Olivia!" JoJo screamed. "Help! Help me! We've got to help Max!"

"I'm coming!" I said.

But there was something I needed to do first.

I turned to the counter. My eyes darted around, back and forth, searching, searching—

There.

Tucked at the back of the counter beneath the cupboard was a big thermos. We have a few of them, as Dad will fill them with coffee or soup and take them with him on his long trips.

I dropped the ladle into the chili, grabbed the thermos, and unscrewed the lid. Then, I picked up the ladle and began carefully scooping chili into the thermos.

"Olivia!" JoJo shrieked.

"I'm coming!" I shouted. "Hang on!"

"Hurry! I need help!"

I finished filling the thermos. I was about to race into my bedroom with it when I saw something else on the counter:

An empty pitcher.

It was the pitcher we used for fruit juice, but it was empty and upside down, tucked beneath the counter and the cookie jar.

I placed the thermos on the counter and grabbed the pitcher. In one swift motion I dunked it into the slow cooker and pulled it out, filling it almost to the top with hot, steaming chili.

"OLIVIA!"

"Coming!" I shouted.

I dropped the ladle into the slow cooker and spun. There was still glass all over the floor from the broken sliding glass door, and I nearly lost my footing as I rounded the corner. But the hallway floor is carpeted, and that made walking easier. Or, I should say jogging, because in three giant leaps—careful ones, as I was carrying the pitcher of chili—I was at my bedroom door. I pushed it open with my free hand.

At the window, JoJo was struggling with Max as he tried to climb through the window. Problem was, Max was bigger than JoJo, and she wasn't strong enough to pull him through. And the window was high enough off the ground that Max couldn't leap through. He would have to pull himself up and through, and he couldn't do it on his own.

And now he had another problem.

A giant green algae monster suddenly appeared from behind him.

"Aaaahhhhh!" Max wailed. *"Help me!"*

I had one chance—and one chance only—to save Max's life.

27

"Watch out!" I shouted. My words were intended for JoJo, but I don't think she heard or knew what I meant. She was struggling to get Max through the window, but I knew that her situation was hopeless—especially now, with the arrival of the green monster.

I raced to the window. Just as the lime-colored beast was reaching out to grab Max's legs, I threw the chili all over him.

The effect it had was immediate, and the same as what had happened in the kitchen. The creature recoiled as the chili splattered all over him. Smoke boiled and churned as the liquid burned its thick, green skin. In seconds, the beast had collapsed into nothing more than a harmless blob, a lumpy puddle of smoldering gelatin.

I placed the empty pitcher on the floor and grabbed one of Max's arms. JoJo and I pulled and pulled until Max tumbled into my bedroom.

"Oh, man!" Max said, seated on the floor and gasping for breath. "Oh, man! That was close! Too close!"

I stepped around Max and leaned out the window. JoJo joined me, and Max, still catching his breath, stood. The three of us gazed down at the pile of chunky green stew, covering the grass. It looked like someone had poured a giant bowl of lime jelly in our yard next to our house.

"What was in that pitcher?" JoJo asked.

"My mom's chili surprise," I said.

"Well, that's what I call a 'surprise,'" said JoJo.

"Your mom's chili did *that?*" Max said, eyes wide.

I nodded.

"How did you find that out?" he asked. "How did you know the chili would stop the thing?"

I nodded. "Out there in the kitchen," I replied.

"One of them—not the one that chased you—came into the house and ate my phone, and—"

"—it *ate* your *phone?*" JoJo said.

Again, I nodded. "It ate my phone. The whole thing. I got really mad, and I didn't know what else to do. So, I scooped up a spoonful of Mom's chili with a soup ladle and threw it all over him. It killed him. Or, I *think* it killed him. If it was even alive in the first place."

"How much of your mom's chili is left?" JoJo asked.

"I'm not sure," I replied. "But there's still some in the slow cooker."

"Looks like we're going to need it," JoJo said, nodding. "Especially if we don't have your phone."

I looked up. Farther down the road, a green blob was emerging from the drainage ditch.

"It's like an invasion," Max said. "They're probably here to take over the world!"

As crazy as it sounded, I couldn't prove that Max was wrong. We still had no idea what the green things were, where they came from, or what they wanted. Yes, I was sure they were made of some sort of algae—the same algae we'd spotted on the ground after the truck rolled over the day before. And if what the driver said was true, then the algae had spent time in space. Somehow, something in space had affected the algae, making it come alive. Or maybe it was as we'd thought when we saw the creature split in two. Maybe it was some sort of space virus or bacteria or something.

But, at the moment, none of that mattered. Without my phone to call for help, we were on our own. We had to figure out what to do to survive as long as we could. Sooner or later, help would arrive. But I knew that Mom would be coming back soon, and she would have no idea what was going on. She would be in a lot of danger and not even know it.

I picked up the pitcher from the floor. "Come on," I said. "We've got some other bowls and stuff in the kitchen that we can fill."

"Too bad we don't have a squirt gun," Max said.

"That would be a good idea," I said, "but the chili is too thick. It would probably jam up the plastic mechanism."

I stopped at my bedroom door and peered down the hall, both ways.

"Be careful," I said quietly. "We have no idea

how many there are, or where they might be."

The three of us tiptoed down the hall and into the kitchen. Our shoes crunched on the broken glass.

"My mom is going to freak when she finds out the sliding glass door is shattered," I said. "There's glass everywhere."

"I think we have bigger problems than your mom freaking out," JoJo said.

She was right, of course. We may have discovered that Mom's special concoction stopped the green monsters, and the three of us each had a supply of her chili: I had the pitcher, while JoJo and Max each had bowls filled with the stuff. There was still some left in the slow cooker, but not very much.

But our troubles were far from over.

28

"We're going to have to be careful not to use up all the chili right away," I said. "This is all we've got."

"Doesn't your mom have any more in the fridge?" JoJo asked. "Whenever my mom makes anything like that, she always makes a ton extra. She'll put it in the fridge or can a bunch of it and put it in the pantry."

I shook my head. "No," I said. "I think this is it. I think the only thing my mom cans are her vegetables."

"How much of this stuff does it take to kill one of those things?" Max asked.

"I'm not sure," I said.

"Maybe all we need is a little bit," JoJo said. "Maybe just a spoonful. That might make it last longer. We don't have any idea how many of those things are out there, and we need to be sure we don't run out of this stuff."

I opened the utensil drawer and pulled out a big spoon. "This should work," I said. "We can give it a try. Maybe we can just fling a little on one of the monsters and see what happens. If it doesn't work, we can pour a bunch more on it."

Max's eyes flared. He pointed. "There's one, right there!" he cried.

In the back yard, a creature had appeared. It was ambling about aimlessly, not seeming to know where it was going, not having any particular direction.

"I'm thinking more and more that these things are like giant, single organisms," I said. "Like single cells or viruses."

"Like giant bugs," JoJo said.

"Maybe," I agreed. "Giant green space bugs."

"Got any bug spray?" Max asked, and he laughed.

"Probably somewhere," I said. "I hope we don't

have to use it, because I don't know where it is."

"Well, get ready," JoJo said. "I think we're going to have to use some chili pretty quick."

We watched as the giant green blob stumbled about in the yard. It was the first time I was able to get a good look and observe one of the beasts without panicking. That doesn't mean I wasn't afraid at the moment, but it felt better to not only have two friends with me, but to have weapons to fight back. Yes, chili was an unlikely weapon...but it worked, and that's all that mattered.

The green goblin came closer to the house.

"JoJo," I said, "get on the other side of the sliding glass door. If that thing comes in here, use a spoonful of chili. We'll watch what happens. If we need more chili to kill it, I'll be on this side of the sliding glass door, and I'll dump my pitcher on it."

"Let's hope that a spoonful will do the trick," JoJo said.

"Let's hope he just goes away," said Max.

"I don't think that's going to happen," I said. "Somehow, they know we're here. Maybe they can smell us. Get ready...he's coming closer."

JoJo got into position on the other side of the

sliding glass door. Of course, there was no glass in it—just the metal frame. Warm air wafted into the kitchen, and again I wondered how I was going to explain everything to Mom.

Then I thought of something else.

How will Mom explain this to Dad? I wondered. While Dad was traveling, he called every night. Mom and I took turns talking to him, and Travis did, too…if he was home. But he was working a lot these days, now that it was summer, and he didn't have to go to school.

I could only imagine how Mom would explain all of this to Dad. *Yes, honey, you're not going to believe this, but we were attacked by giant green monsters from outer space. They broke the sliding glass door, and there was glass and green goo all over the place. But thanks to Olivia and her friends—and my chili surprise—we're all safe. So…how is your trip going?*

That conversation, however, might not ever take place. First, we had to survive.

"Here he comes!" JoJo said as she scooped up a spoonful of chili. *"Get ready!"*

29

JoJo and I waited on opposite sides of the shattered sliding glass door. Meanwhile, Max, carrying his bowl, ducked around the corner and out of sight.

The hideous green monster shuffled toward our house. It stepped up onto the cement porch, then stopped and looked around, as if searching for something. For a moment, it appeared to be sniffing the air, but I couldn't be sure. It didn't look like the thing had much of a nose—if any nose at all.

JoJo looked at me, and mouthed the words *are you ready?*

I nodded in reply, indicating that I was. Which wasn't really true. How can you be ready for a giant green beast from outer space that wants to eat you?

The monster moved, coming toward the house. I could see JoJo tense up, waiting on the opposite side of the broken sliding glass door, bowl of chili tucked beneath one arm, spoonful of chili in the other, ready for battle. She certainly didn't look like she was about to square off with a giant green jelly beast that was four times her size. She looked like she was just playing around, goofing off.

Just as the algae monster reached the door, JoJo flung the spoonful of chili. Then, she took a step back, putting a little more distance between herself and the creature.

But the best news of all?

The tiny amount of chili had a powerful effect. Just the small splattering stopped the green monster in its tracks as it stood at the edge of the sliding glass door. The small droplets of chili burned and caused small swirls of smoke to rise from the places where it came in contact with the creature, which began to tremble and shake. Within seconds, its body had turned into a steaming pile of green mush on the porch. Some of the green residue seeped over the frame of the doorway and spilled inside.

"It worked!" JoJo cried. "Just a little bit is all we need!"

Max came out from the hall where he'd been hiding. He was looking beyond JoJo, into the yard. "Well, we'd better stay ready," he said. "Here comes another one."

I turned and looked into the back yard, where another green mass of jelly had appeared.

"Where are they all coming from?" Max asked.

"They must be reproducing on their own," JoJo said.

"That means there could be a lot more," I said.

"Yeah, well, let's hope not," said Max, nodding toward the empty slow cooker. "What we have in these bowls is all we have left. I hope it's enough."

Enough until when? I wondered. *With my phone gone, we had no way of contacting anyone. Yes, I'm sure Mom received my panicked message, but—*

My thought was interrupted by another thought altogether.

"Oh, my gosh!" I said. "I can't believe I didn't think about this before!"

"What?" JoJo asked.

"Our computer!" I said. "We can get a message

to someone that way! You guys stay here and guard the kitchen!"

Without explaining further, I hustled through the kitchen, still carrying the full pitcher of chili. I hurried down the hallway and into a room Mom and Dad called 'the office.' Actually, it was just a spare bedroom that was never used for guests. At one time, there was a single bed in it. But, as Mom and Dad began to use it more and more as a place to work, they finally dismantled the bed and donated it to a local thrift store. Now the room had a desk and a big, comfy office chair on rollers. There was a bookshelf against the wall filled with papers and file folders. A large, flat screen monitor sat on the desk with the box on the floor.

I sat down at the desk and placed my right hand on the mouse. The computer screen burst to life, but just as I was about to log on—

Pop!

The sound came from somewhere inside the house.

On the desk, the computer screen went dark.

What the heck?

"Hey!" I heard JoJo shout from the kitchen. "I

think we just lost power!"

"Oh, no!" I yelled back. "I didn't even have time to contact anyone!"

I moved the mouse back and forth, thinking that, somehow, magically, the computer would work.

Of course not, I thought. *There's no power.*

I heaved a sigh.

Think, Olivia, think.

It was hard not to feel overwhelmed and frustrated. The three of us were all alone, battling something we knew very little about. Yes, we were fortunate to find out that Mom's chili was so powerful and could be used against the creatures…but it wasn't going to last long. I wondered if there was anything else we could use. Maybe the creatures would have the same reaction to milk or orange juice, or something simple like that.

Problem is, if it didn't work, we'd be in a lot of trouble. I had been really lucky to discover the chili had the effects that it did. That had been by accident because I was mad and was out of options. I'd thrown chili at the creature simply out of frustration.

Now, we had another problem: the power had gone out.

What had caused it? Was it something the green algae creatures had done? Most likely. We had no idea what they were capable of or what they wanted.

Then, I heard a sound in the distance. Faint, but growing louder.

A siren! A siren! Help was coming! Help was finally on the way!

Then, another sound.

From the kitchen.

Screaming.

Max and JoJo.

30

I raced from the computer room, carrying the pitcher of chili in my left hand, holding it in front of me as I rushed down the hall. I stopped when I reached the kitchen.

Max and JoJo were standing near the shattered sliding glass door. Both of their chili bowls were empty. Beyond the door was a mountain of green slime that appeared to be melting before my very eyes. It was smoldering and smoking, making hot crackling and popping sounds.

"What happened?" I asked.

"There were three of them," Max said. "They all came at us at once."

"They came at us, and I threw the whole bowl at them," JoJo said.

"Me, too," Max said. "I thought I would need more than a spoonful."

Now we had a problem: our chili supply was low.

However, the siren I'd heard was even louder, closer to our house.

I spun and walked to the living room window. Outside, on the highway, a large, red fire engine had stopped. I could see the dark shadows of two figures on the front behind the windshield.

And emerging from the ditch?

A giant green monster.

"Let's go!" I shouted. "We can stop him!"

By then, Max and JoJo had joined me at my side.

"What if that thing attacks us?" Max asked.

"I've still got a full pitcher of chili," I said, raising the large plastic container. "If I need to, I can use it. But I don't see any in our yard. All I see is the one out there in the ditch. If he attacks us, we can use the chili to stop him. But we've got to make it to the fire truck. Then, we'll be safe."

"How do you know?" JoJo asked.

It was a good question. Truth was, I didn't know. I was just assuming we'd be safe. I guess I'd always figured that when the police or fire or other emergency responders arrived on the scene, everything was going to be okay. Of course, that wasn't always the case. But it sure felt better, safer, knowing that professional help had arrived.

"I guess I don't know for sure," I said. "But I know we'll be safer with them." I nodded toward the fire truck. "Those men and women are trained to handle situations like this."

"How do you train to handle bloodthirsty green monsters from outer space?" Max asked.

It was another good question.

"Well, we all know we can't stay here. This is the last of the chili. We'll be much safer when we make it to the fire truck. And like I said, if we need to, we can use this chili. Now…let's stop talking about it and get moving!"

I raced to the front door, which had been left open by Max. I pushed open the screen door, carefully looking all around: in the yard, the driveway, out by the shed, and the garage.

"I don't see any," I said, pushing the screen all the way open and stepping onto the porch. "Come on!"

Carrying the pitcher of chili, I hurried across the porch, down the short flight of steps, and into the yard. JoJo and Max were on my heels. All three of us looked around warily, nervous, tense.

I started jogging. I couldn't go very fast, but the good thing about Mom's chili is that it's thick and goopy, and when I ran it didn't splash like water or juice or other thin liquids. I could jog—not very fast, mind you—without worrying of spilling the chili from the pitcher.

Up ahead, the fire truck was parked in the middle of the road. Atop it was a long light bar, flashing red, pulsating in quick rhythm. The two figures were still seated in the front seat.

But the green algae monster had scrambled up the ditch and was attacking the vehicle! The creature was trying to push it, and, although it wasn't big enough to knock over the truck, it was rocking the truck from side to side. I imagined that the two people seated inside were probably horrified, wondering what on earth was happening, what was attacking them.

But I had a pitcher of chili…and a plan.

31

I picked up my pace, breaking from a jog into a run as I carried the pitcher. Although it wasn't very heavy, I'd been carrying it with one hand for a few minutes, and I could feel the muscles in my wrist and forearm beginning to burn. I slowed for a moment and switched the pitcher of chili to my other hand, then picked up my pace again.

Max and Olivia were running at my side, matching my strides.

"I don't think we should be running toward that thing!" Max said.

"We can stop it with the chili!" I said. "There's only one of them!"

"Yeah, for now!" JoJo said. "What happens if that thing splits in two?"

"Then there will be two of them," I said as I ran. "That's why we've got to stop it now. It doesn't look like the people in the fire truck know what to do."

As soon as I said those words, the passenger door of the fire truck opened. A man dressed in bulky, firefighting gear jumped out and ran to the back of the truck. The driver slid over and out, and he, too, ran to the back of the truck and out of sight.

And on the other side of the truck, the green algae monster continued to push the vehicle. It was relentless, as though it really believed it might succeed in turning the vehicle onto its side. Thankfully, the creature was no match for the stationary fire truck, which had to weigh several tons.

Then, the creature turned and backed away from the vehicle. A large spray of water was hitting it, but it didn't seem to be having much of an effect. I imagined that the firefighters were using their hose to try to stop the beast, but the only effect it was having was a distraction. The high-pressure stream of water didn't seem to do anything at all to the green monsters.

"You guys stay back," I said. "I'm going to run up and dump this chili on that thing."

"I'm going with you," JoJo said.

"Me, too," Max replied.

I didn't have time to argue. Besides, I was sure that as soon as I dumped the chili on the creature, it would crumble into a heaping mass of steamy, green jelly.

Meanwhile, the spray of water only succeeded in stopping the beast from attacking the fire truck. He turned to face the heavy stream, then turned again…and saw the three of us approaching. Probably figuring that we were much easier prey, the green thing began coming toward us.

We stopped. I held the pitcher of chili ready as the green goblin came toward us.

And he was gigantic! By far, it was the biggest one I'd seen so far. I was sure it was the same creature that had attacked me earlier, the same one that attacked JoJo as well as the passing car.

Had it grown bigger in that short amount of time? I wondered.

"It's like a giant green gorilla," JoJo said. "If that's the same one that attacked me, he's gotten a lot bigger."

Although I was armed with a pitcher of chili and I was certain the liquid would work, I couldn't help but to be frightened by lingering doubts and niggling questions, nagging and poking at me.

What if the chili doesn't work this time? I thought. *I'm going to have to get close to the thing to splash the liquid on it. What if, for some reason, it doesn't have the same effect as before?*

I couldn't think about that. I had to push those thoughts away and be confident. If I got scared now, I might lose focus on what I needed to do. And I couldn't afford to do that. My life—and the lives of JoJo and Max—depended on it.

The beast lumbered toward me, towering like a fat skyscraper. I was barely aware of the two firemen at the back of the truck. They had stopped spraying water at the creature when they found it had no effect, and they were now watching it come toward me.

And what did I do?

I started walking toward the green slime creature, holding my pitcher of chili close to my chest, ready to throw the liquid. I didn't want to get too close, but I had to get within my own throwing distance. I couldn't afford to miss, even though I was certain it would only take a little chili to stop the creature.

We approached one another slowly, like two prize fighters in a ring. It was as though the creature sensed danger, and was sizing me up, being cautious. I imagined that it must have looked funny to anyone watching, seeing a girl my size taking on an enormous, green mountain.

"Don't get any closer!" one of the firemen hollered.

"I know what I'm doing!" I shouted back.

But did I, really? Did I really know what I was doing?

No. I could only hope my plan was going to work.

In a few steps, I would be close enough. I drew back the pitcher, ready to unleash the hot chili.

The creature stopped.

I paused.

The beast began to shimmy and shake. It trembled and squirmed.

What in the—?

Then, I realized what was happening.

Cell division was the term I'd learned in school.

The creature was reproducing itself. It was splitting.

And within seconds, the nightmare became all too real.

Now there were *two* of them.

32

I was stunned. Seeing the enormous creature split into two was horrifying, and I knew I had to act fast. I couldn't wait any longer.

I drew back the pitcher and swung it in a wide arc in front of me, taking a step closer as I flung the chili. My goal was to get chili on both of the monsters at the same time. I was sure I had enough chili...all I had to do was make sure my aim was good.

It was.

Mom's chili splattered on both beasts, and the effects were instant. Smoke roiled up, and there were cracking, hissing, and popping sounds. In seconds, the two creatures had been reduced to piles of nothing but green goop.

"Holy cow, Olivia!" Max said from behind me. "You did it! You really did it!"

The firemen had dropped their water hose and were hurrying up to us.

"Are you kids all right?" one of them asked.

"Yeah, we are now," JoJo said.

"At least for the time being," I said. "There's probably more of those things out there."

"Oh, there are, for sure," the other fireman said. "They're all over town."

I was shocked. "All over town?!?!" I echoed.

"Yeah," the other fireman said. "Haven't you heard?"

"We've been trapped in my house," I said. "One of those things ate my phone."

"And the power went out," Max said.

I was still carrying the empty pitcher. Inside, it was stained with the brown residue of Mom's Chili Surprise.

"What was in there?" one of the men asked. He looked curiously at the pitcher and reached out. I handed it to him.

"My mom's chili," I replied.

"We've got to get more of this stuff," the fireman said.

I shook my head. "This was the last of it," I replied. "But if you talk to—"

An approaching car farther up the highway caught my attention. It was heading in our direction. In seconds, I recognized the vehicle.

Mom!

When the firemen saw me staring off into the distance, they turned.

"That's my mom, right there!" I said. "She made the chili!"

By then, Mom was approaching us, and she slowed to a stop. When she saw me, she got out of her car. I ran up to her and gave her a long, tight hug.

"I got your message earlier," she said.

"We were attacked by green monsters, Mrs. Barnes!" Max said. "Honest!"

"We were," I said, looking at Mom. "But we used your chili to stop them!"

Mom looked shocked. "My chili?" she asked.

"I found out that it turned them into mush," I said, pointing at the two smoldering piles of goo—all that was left of the two algae monsters—on the shoulder of the road.

"We'd sure like to know how you made that chili, ma'am," one of the firemen said. "We've got more of those green things poppin' up all over town, and whatever is in your chili seems to be the only thing we've found that will stop them."

So, we all went to our house and Mom made up another huge batch of her chili, using her special recipe of her homegrown Arkansas Night Reaper peppers. She made gallons of the stuff, and the firemen hauled it away and came back for more.

And it worked! We found out later that the firemen were able to put the chili into high-pressure hoses and go around town and get rid of the green algae goblins. It took them a couple of days, but they finally succeeded. The town of Russellville, and everyone in it, was safe. No one was even hurt, which seemed like a miracle.

But the craziest part of this story is what we found out later....

33

While all of this was going on, while emergency responders worked to get rid of the remaining algae monsters, everyone in and around Russellville was told to stay home and remain indoors. Which was kind of a bummer, but not too bad. The power company worked to get our electricity back on the very same day, so at least I had our computer to play around with.

And our suspicions were correct: the 'algae monsters' were just that. Somehow, something contaminated the algae that had been sent into space. How or why this occurred, no one knew just yet. Experts were sure they would find out, but they explained that the 'blobs' were very similar to viruses…which is another thing we'd suspected.

But what was most fascinating was that scientists discovered that Mom's Arkansas Night Reaper peppers contain a compound called capsaicin—which is actually in all chili peppers. It's what makes the peppers hot. Turns out, that's the ingredient that caused the adverse reaction in the algae monsters. Once scientists discovered this, they were able to separate the capsaicin and use it to stop the green globs. It was just a lucky accident that I had discovered this, and it was only out of frustration. I'd only thrown Mom's chili at the green goblin because I was frustrated and mad. It was a simple stroke of luck. I hate to think what might have happened if I had used something else, something that hadn't had the same effect as the chili.

●●●

Later in the summer, when Dad left for a week-long haul that would take him to California and back, Mom and I went to Leesburg, Georgia to visit my uncle—my mom's brother—for a few days. Travis was still working a lot, so he stayed home.

I'd never been to Georgia before. I'd only met my uncle on the times he visited for Thanksgiving or Christmas, when he and my aunt came to Arkansas. But they don't have any kids, so I was thinking that our visit was going to be kind of boring.

Not so.

Turns out, my aunt and uncle have neighbors that have kids my age: a boy, Curtis, and a girl, Shelly. Curtis is my age, and Shelly is a year younger. I liked Curtis instantly. He's a little quiet, but he's not shy. Rather, he thinks a lot. Instead of talking, he thinks about what he wants to say...or what he doesn't want to say. He smiles a lot, and he's someone I liked instantly, someone easy and comfortable to be around.

Of course, I told them all about what had happened to me and Max and JoJo. I told them about how everything started with the truck rolling over, the algae spilling out. I told them about how the green blobs had attacked us, how they grew to gigantic size very quickly, and how they multiplied like cells.

"I heard about that," he said. "It was on the news."

"It's all true," I said. "Me and my friends saw it

187

all. We were really lucky we weren't hurt. Or worse. It's the craziest thing that's ever happened in this country."

Curtis and Shelly looked at each other.

"Oh, I don't know about that," Curtis said.

"What do you mean?" I replied.

"I mean that there are other crazy things that happen," he replied.

"It's just that most don't know about it," Shelly said.

"Or they don't believe it," said Curtis.

"Like what?" I asked.

"Like a pumpkin that came to life," Shelly said.

"A real, live jack-o'-lantern," said Curtis, nodding.

I frowned. "What do you mean by 'real' and 'live?'" I asked.

"Exactly what I said," Curtis replied.

"How does a jack-o'-lantern come to life?" I asked.

"I'll tell you what happened," Curtis said. "But I doubt you'll believe it."

"My friends and I were attacked by killer algae from outer space," I said. "I'll believe just about anything."

"All right," Curtis said. "Here's what happened."

And that's how I found out about the Giant Jack-O'-Lantern of Georgia....

Next:

#45: The Giant Jack-O'-Lantern of Georgia

Continue on for a FREE preview!

1

"Curtis!" my sister shouted. "Slow down! This isn't a race!"

I stopped pedaling, laughed, and turned my head. A few dozen yards behind me, my sister, Shelly, was pumping the pedals of her bike, trying to catch up.

"What's the hurry?" she shouted.

"You're just slow," I said, allowing my bike to coast to a stop on the trail. Shelly stopped. She adjusted her blue bike helmet, then her sunglasses.

"I mean, really," she said. "Why do you have

to go so fast?"

I remained seated on my bike, both hands on the handlebars, one leg on the ground. I shrugged.

"It's your problem if you can't keep up," I said.

"You're a year older," she protested.

"You're almost the same size as me," I replied.

"So?" Shelly said. "Look, just go slower. We don't have to race to Ray's house."

"All right," I said. "You lead the way, and I'll follow you. We can go at your pace."

I moved to the side to let Shelly pass. We began pedaling again, winding our way through the woods. The trail, narrow and winding, was a shortcut from our block to our friend Ray Coopersmith's house. We were going to meet up with him and then go dig for night crawlers on old Hattie Broussard's farm.

And why would we do that?

Well, there's a bait shop not far from where Ray lives, and the guy that owns it buys our night crawlers to sell to fishermen. He gives us ten cents for each night crawler, and we split the money between the three of us. Ten cents for each night crawler might not sound like a lot, but with the three of us—Shelly, Ray, and myself—working together, we can sometimes gather up dozens of night crawlers in just a short time. Of course, it all depends on our hunting grounds, the weather, the time of year, things like that. But on an October day like today? Perfect. It was warm, and rain had fallen heavily overnight. Most likely, night crawlers would be near the surface of the ground, making them easier to find and catch.

And, of course, there was no place better to hunt for night crawlers than old Hattie Broussard's field. It used to be a pumpkin farm, years ago. My dad told me that, long ago, it had been one of the biggest pumpkin farms in the state. No one had planted anything or tended to it in years. Old Hattie Broussard—nobody knew how old she really was—lived in the family farmhouse all by herself. I'd heard that her husband had died a few years ago, which was sad.

But she didn't seem lonely. Hattie was very nice, and she let us dig for night crawlers in the huge field whenever wanted. Once in a while, Ray's mom would bake some cookies that we would take to Hattie as a 'thank you' for allowing us to dig in her field. She really seemed to enjoy the cookies.

So, that was our plan. We were on our way to meet up with Ray. From his house, we'd ride our bikes along an old, weathered two-track road—another shortcut through the woods—to the Broussard farm. Just like we did last week, and the week before that. It was a warm, October day, the conditions were perfect, and I was hopeful that we'd find gobs and gobs of night crawlers.

And we would. We'd find tons of night crawlers.

And…

Night*mares.*

2

Old Hattie Broussard didn't like October.

She sat in an ancient, squeaky rocking chair on the long front porch that filled the eastern side of the house.

Watching.

Sipping cold sweet tea.

Watching.

Her thick, curly hair had once been jet-black, but it had turned gray long ago. She was thin, as she had always been, and she was tall. Her bones and muscles were still tight and strong, but not as much as they had been. She moved slower these days, but she didn't mind.

It was early October. Years ago, this would have been harvest time. The fields would have been busy with workers, oh, so busy, cutting pumpkins from their stalks and bringing them to a special area near the barn.

Thousands of pumpkins.

People came from miles around to buy them. People cooked and baked with them, making pumpkin bread, pumpkin muffins, pumpkin cookies, and—of course—pumpkin pies.

But probably one of their most popular uses were for the making of pumpkin carvings.

Jack-o'-lanterns.

Hattie Broussard rocked gently in her chair. She looked across the enormous field, now over-grown with wild grass and scrub brush. Far away, among the tangle of tall grass and weeds, an old scarecrow, torn and shredded by time and weather, hung from a pole in the field.

Hattie squinted, deep in thought. When was

the last year pumpkins had been grown and harvested? Twenty years ago? Thirty? She wasn't sure. At some point, the farm had closed down. Workers were let go, operations stopped. No more pumpkins had been planted. No more fall harvests.

But there was more to it than that.

Something had happened one night, many years ago. Something so terrible that she'd blocked it from her memory, storing the horrible images and recollections from that night, locking them away somewhere in her brain, in a dark place she hadn't thought about, wouldn't think about, *couldn't* think about.

What was it? What had happened all those years ago?

She couldn't remember.

What she *could* remember was that something had happened, long, long ago. Far, far back in time when she had been a little girl.

On Halloween.

She shuddered. The day was warm, but she suddenly felt a chill crawl through her body.

Why?

It was early October. Summer had ended in September, pushed out by a bustling, insistent autumn. The season spoke from the rattle of leaves in the wind. It whispered through the tall grass in the field. Hattie felt fall in the air as it touched her face on the afternoons she sat on her porch, watching, watching...

And once in a while, a vision came to her. Just a quick glimpse of a horrifying, simple image.

A carved pumpkin.

A jack-o'-lantern.

With menacing eyes and rows of sharp, threatening teeth.

Glowing from within by an unseen candle.

The vision was hideous and terrifying. These days, it appeared less and less in her mind.

But Halloween was coming.

Again.

October 31st would soon arrive.

She sipped her tea, then returned her gaze to the field.

She felt nervous. Anxious. Tense.

Something was happening.

What?

She didn't know.

But she knew, somehow, that *something* was coming.

He was coming. She knew he was.

He was coming... *back.*

Soon, it would be Halloween.

Soon, he would be here...

ABOUT THE AUTHOR

Johnathan Rand has authored more than 100 books for children and adults since the year 2000, with over 6 million copies in print. His series include the incredibly popular *AMERICAN CHILLERS, MICHIGAN CHILLERS, FREDDIE FERNORTNER-FEARLESS FIRST GRADER, THE ADVENTURE CLUB, DOLLAR $TORE DANNY*, and the all-new *NIGHTMARE NATION* series.When not traveling, Rand lives in northern Michigan with his wife and adopted shelter dogs. He is also the only author in the world to have a store that sells only his works: **CHILLERMANIA** is located in Indian River, Michigan, and is open year round. Johnathan Rand is not always at the store, but he has been known to drop by frequently. Find out more at:

WWW.AMERICANCHILLERS.COM

ATTENTION YOUNG AUTHORS!
DON'T MISS

If you want to sharpen your writing skills, become a better writer, and have a blast, Johnathan Rand's Author Quest is for you!

Designed exclusively for young writers, Author Quest is 4 days/3 nights of writing courses, instruction, and classes in the secluded wilds of northern lower Michigan. Oh, there are lots of other fun indoor and outdoor activities, too . . . but the main focus of Author Quest is about becoming an even better writer! Instructors include published authors and (of course!) Johnathan Rand. No matter what kind of writing you enjoy: fiction, non-fiction, fantasy, thriller/horror, humor, mystery, history . . . this camp is designed for writers who have this in common: they LOVE to write, and they want to improve their skills!

For complete details and an application, visit:

www.americanchillers.com

AUTOGRAPHED COPIES
OF ALL

AMERICAN
CHILLERS
AMERICA's #1 SERIES FOR MAXIMUM CHILLS!

CAN BE FOUND AT:
WWW.AMERICANCHILLERS.COM

All AudioCraft Publishing, Inc. books are proudly printed, bound, and manufactured in the United States of America, utilizing American resources, labor, and materials.